THE MYSTERY OF THE AMERICAN SLUG

A Lady Darriby-Jones Mystery

CM RAWLINS

CleanTales Publishing

Copyright © CleanTales Publishing

First published in October 2023

All characters and events in this publication, other than those clearly in the public domain, are fictitious and any resemblance to real persons, living or dead, is purely coincidental.

Copyright © CleanTales Publishing

The moral right of the author has been asserted.

All rights reserved. This book or any portion thereof may not be reproduced or used in any manner whatsoever without the express written permission of the publisher except for the use of brief quotations in a book review.

For questions and comments about this book, please contact info@cleantales.com

ISBN: 9798864647271
Imprint: Independently Published

Other books in the A Lady Darriby-Jones Mystery series

The Mystery of the Polite Man

The Mystery of the American Slug

The Mystery of the Back Passage

The Mystery of the Missing Doctor

A Lady Darriby-Jones Mystery

BOOK TWO

Chapter One

Lady Darriby-Jones ached for a pink gin. When she closed her eyes, she saw the heavy cut of the glasses Torino liked to serve it in. Yet, when she opened them again, there was no such glass within reach, just a thousand people congratulating her on an excellent slug symposium.

"All credit to my husband and Sir John Plumer," she would say, over and over again, as she steered her way towards the library; if Torino was absent, she would jolly well pour her own, however put out he would later be.

It had been a long few days, but at least Darriby was a happy man. She spotted him at that moment by the library door; perhaps he had the same plan of action as she had, substituting a good malt for pink gin but otherwise the same objective. He even had his left hand on the library door handle, while the right was exercised in continually pumping some inappropriately dressed individuals who looked loud, although the constant hum of people up and down the halls and corridors made it impossible to be sure whether their voices lived up to their looks.

"Yes, Alfie, closing stages now, soon be quiet again," she said on seeing Alfie Burrows, the private secretary she had gone to Oxford and brought back to work for her husband, cutting up slugs and noting down every little detail and then organising the myriad of slugs on every horizontal surface in the East Wing of Darriby Hall.

"I was hoping for a quiet word, Lady Darriby-Jones." She looked at him, saw the worry on his face, knew what caused it.

"Lord Darriby-Jones spoke most highly of your work, just this very morning," she replied.

"I was concerned that he might dispense with my services as the symposium is coming to an end."

"Far from it, dear boy. Your temporary contract is to be made permanent and I do believe there's a rise in the offing."

"Well, that's delightful, thank you, Lady..."

"You've earned it, my boy, even more so with your extra-curricular activities of recent days." That was a reference to the case just closed that she called the Mystery of the Polite Man. She had solved the case, despite the efforts of DCI 'Rude' Manners, but Alfie Burrows had played a strong supporting role; his name would be on the screen right below hers. Well, politeness dictated that her daughter, Lady Alice Darriby-Jones, go before him, making him third in the credit listing. Frank Hoosish had been exposed as the wicked, jealous murderer of poor Matthew Carter, a war hero just seeking a quiet life. She was convinced his death was an accident but as long as Hoosish remained at large, slipping through the net of police custody despite Lady Darriby-Jones handing the man over on a platter, he would appear to all the world as a murderer; that would rank in people's minds even more than the fact that he was half-Darriby.

Enough of past mysteries. Who knew what today would bring? Well, too many people lingering far too long and separating Lady Darriby-Jones from her pink gin.

"Be a dear, Alfie, and help me rid Lord Darriby-Jones of his hangers-on. They're preventing me from getting to my gin."

"Of course, Lady Darriby-Jones. It will be my pleasure." Only, it wasn't as easy as he expected for one simple reason.

The small knot of people surrounding Lord Darriby-Jones were Americans. Alfie tried valiantly for a moment while Lady Darriby-Jones hung back, but it soon became apparent that the big guns were needed.

"Excuse me, ladies and gents, but you're blocking my way to the gin decanter." That was an excellent opening shot, but the volley back was even better.

"I don't mind if I do, thanks Lady Darriby-Jones. Which way to the decanter? I'm a Scotch man myself, but where there's gin in a gentleman's home there will always be whisky not too far away."

"You better come in then. Who are you, by the way?" Might as well be civil to the enemy, even if his twang was unbearable.

"Al Hammerstein, ma'am." His hand shot out.

"I'm not the queen." She did not have the remotest possibility of royal blood in her veins, but didn't want to make the point too forcibly. Then she saw that she would have to explain if she kept up her antagonism and the real objective wasn't this skirmish but the capture of said gin decanter.

"Professor Al Hammerstein of S.T.I.N.K., and this is my..."

"What did you say? Stink? You're a professor of unpleasant smells?"

"No, ma'am, it stands for the Science and Technology Institute of North Kakama. That's our college based in Kakama, Washington State, real close to Seattle. You've heard of Seattle, ain't ya?" Lady Darriby-Jones hadn't but let it go.

"More introductions, please," she said instead.

"This here is my wife, Mrs Hammerstein." Why did people introduce their wife with the obvious 'Mrs', Lady Darriby-Jones wondered as she held out her hand for the obligatory handshakes. Mrs Hammerstein was clearly not American, heralding from either Liverpool or the midlands; those accents always confused her.

The rest of Hammerstein's entourage consisted of two contrasting figures. Mr Harrison B Potters was loud and garish, wearing, of all things, a sports jacket over heavily creased flannels that gave him a sailor look. She wanted to reach out and turn down the volume knob every time he spoke, which was often and without much consciousness of his surroundings.

"I'm a PhD student," he said. "Subject is the love life of the common black slug." Lady Darriby-Jones felt able to switch off at that moment; at least Darriby's slug-talk steered clear of intimacy between Mr and Mrs Slug.

The fourth person was much easier to accept, although her timidity made it tough to remember her. Miss Betty Bollinger had a sweet, shy smile and it seemed that behind the smile lay more of the same.

"Dear," Lord Darriby-Jones said, "these lovely people were just asking about staying to conduct some studies and I was explaining that it's a bit of a tall order right now with all the refurbishments planned for the next few months."

"Quite, dear, quite so."

"Please hear us out, noble lord and lady," Hammerstein said as the small party moved through the library door and into Torino's welcoming arms. Lady Darriby-Jones felt suddenly close to her objective; certainly, she'd collected a bunch of hangers-on but that was life, happened all the time.

The American professor had a proposal. Armed with a chunky glass of malt, he let loose on the type of horse-trading the Darriby-Joneses were not at all used to.

"Sir and lady," he started, illustrating, once again, the average American's incredible inability to address aristocrats correctly, "I understand it's an awkward time but we're keen as mustard to get stuck into the veritable slug city we have here." He spread his hands wide, as if the slugs were right there in the library, camping out on the bookshelves and sneaking glugs of gin and Scotch.

"I'm afraid it's..."

"Wait sir, wait until you hear just how much we appreciate coming to stay a week or two. We've got in our possession something you might be mighty interested in."

"What would that be, Hammerstein?"

"Why, no more than a real rare version of the banana slug species." He turned to Lady Darriby-Jones and added in a quieter voice, "that's Ariolimax columbianus, ma'am." Lady Darriby-Jones found herself nodding in receipt of his words.

"You don't mean the...?" Lord Darriby-Jones suddenly sat bolt upright in his seat.

"Well, if you're thinking of the Square Nosed Banana Slug, then I'm happy to report we do have one of these rare 'n beautiful slugs in our collection. Banana slugs are the predominant variety in our part of the world. The Olympic Forest Reserve was set up to help preserve many aspects of local fauna and flora. But the squared-nosed cousin of the common banana slug is a real rare item."

"Excellent, excellent. Can I see it? Do you have it with you, Hammerstein?" Darriby was now out of his chair, moving from foot to foot like a small child in need of the little room.

"We can send for it. I could call my department this very minute. The little beauty can travel by train to New York, first-class of course, from there it's only a matter of days to London, say two weeks door to door." He was getting ready for his knockout blow. "And that's all the time we need to stay here. Just two weeks and we'll be out of yer hair, Lord Darriby."

"You mean you would do that for me?"

"For the king of the slug symposium? For sure."

"I'm not sure," Lady Darriby-Jones said into the following silence, not quite knowing whether she objected on principle or was negotiating on behalf of her husband. "You see, we can't hold up the refurbishment of the main house and were planning to go away to Scotland for a few months." After all, a slug was a slug; who would sell their privacy for a sighting of some obscure variety?

Then the absolute knockout blow hit the room, with Professor Hammerstein saying there must be some confusion; The Square Nosed Banana Slug was to be a gift, not a loan, to form the centrepiece of the Darriby collection.

That left Lady Darriby-Jones isolated; even Alfie would want to see this fine specimen with its square nose and bulging eyes, or whatever features it boasted.

"When would you like to arrive?" she asked.

"There's no time like the present," Hammerstein replied. "How about we wrap things up at the Darriby Arms and move our gear over in the morning?"

Chapter Two

True to Hammerstein's word, the American team moved in after breakfast on Monday, in fact, indecently early; Lady Darriby-Jones was a habitual early riser, yet would never dream of imposing herself on others before elevenses at the earliest. While Torino and the staff didn't issue a word of complaint about the extra work, coming hard on the heels of the symposium, Lady Darriby-Jones had three reasons to be glum. She felt guilty about the imposition on the servants, who had worked their socks off (odd expression, she thought, but it sounded about right). She didn't want the disruption herself, feeling rather fatigued after both the symposium and the dramatic events leading up to the capture of Frank Hoosish. Finally, she loved Darriby Hall and everything about the estate, but sometimes one needs a change and she was rather looking forward to a couple of months on their Scottish estate while the decorators did their bit with plaster and paint.

Then she looked at her husband and saw the huge smile of anticipation at the prospect of ownership of his very own greater squared face or whatever the blighter went by. She knew then it couldn't be any other way.

"It's a favour for his lordship," she told Torino, very much appreciating the patience and endurance of the strange Italian butler who had attached themselves to the Darriby-Joneses a few years ago when they had travelled to Pisa in search of a slug unique to that area. Torino actually leant a bit, just like the famous tower he could see from the bedroom window of the house he had grown up in.

"I have grave news, milady," he replied, his light Italian voice trying hard to sound grave.

For a moment, Lady Darriby-Jones thought Torino might be handing in his notice, deciding to spend the rest of his days running a bed-and-breakfast where the waves crashed against the rocks and the locals spoke in strange ways about ghosts and ghoulies.

"It's Mrs Stone," he said when urged by her to spit it out.

"Surely not?" This was even more serious than Torino packing his bags and heading for the sunset.

"Her mother's ill, milady. She needs to be away for a while, but I believe I have a solution, milady."

Lady Darriby-Jones had once been forced by her father to listen to a speech made by some visiting Australian businessman in coal, the same trade as her father. He had colourful clothes and an even more colourful vocab. The speech had centred on a single lesson:

> *Don't bring a problem to your boss, bring a solution to the problem you aren't bringing to their attention.*

Clearly, Torino had heard the same Aussie entrepreneur and taken the lesson to heart.

"I understand, milady, that the Everetts are away for a few months, gone to New York for their daughter's wedding. They're not taking Mrs Britain with them, milady."

"But she's a terrible cook, Torino!" Surely, he could do better than that? Lady Darriby-Jones remembered a dinner party at Selby Court a few years back. They had staggered back to the Rolls and had to stop several times en route home.

"I'm afraid every other cook is engaged for the season, milady."

"So be it, Torino, so be it." They could hardly starve, although with Mrs Britain in charge of the kitchens, they probably would.

―――

"Morning guys," Harrison B Potters said on entering through the perpetually sticking front door into the main hall, with its long gallery doubling back on the main part of the staircase. The gallery, hung with pictures, including both a Rembrandt and one of a horse done by Lady Alice, aged six and three quarters, led to a tiny door. Twenty years earlier, on first arriving at Darriby Hall as a slender and wide-eyed bride, she had fitted easily through the little door to the myriad of rooms that lay beyond, a house within a house. Now, her eyes were just as wide, perhaps a bit warmer too, but two decades of Mrs Stone's game stew and apple pie had made it somewhat harder to squeeze through any small gap, this one being no exception.

Regardless of this, she led the Americans through and personally allocated bed space in the large, ancient rooms beyond.

"I believe Lord Darriby-Jones has allocated space in the west sitting room where he does most of his own work." That was a late insistence by Lady Darriby-Jones. Truth was, Darriby did most of his work in the library, where Alfie Burrows also had a desk, but that doubled as Lady Darriby-Jones's 'pink gin' room and she wasn't going to give that up in a hurry. Consequently, the footmen plus a contingent of gardeners had moved Lord Darriby-Jones's work desk out of the library late that night, returning early in the morning to move Alfie's desk across.

Then, her conscience struck her straight across the bows. She wasn't being at all friendly and that broke the Darriby tradition like a knife carving through a lamb joint.

"Perhaps you can join me for a drink in the library at noon. Lord Darriby-Jones likes to have his lunch promptly at one, so that will give us an hour to get acquainted."

―――

Harrison B Potters, apparently, didn't or couldn't wait for the appointed hour to get acquainted. He dumped his two suitcases on the bed of the room allocated him and went in search of the 'chick that's never out of her jodhpurs', perhaps hoping to remove those jodhpurs himself.

He caught up with his quarry on the side stairs a few moments later, impressing her immediately with his knowledge of horses. Lady Darriby-Jones, coming down the stairs at the same moment, but a flight above, stopped when she heard their voices.

"Perhaps you'll take me out one day," he suggested with a confidence that would leave Alfie standing.

"Sure thing," Lady Alice replied, evidently thinking that a suitable response for an American. "Tell me, do you ride Western style or English?"

"English all the way, honey. I get a real ribbing but always say English's the only way."

Lady Darriby-Jones, on the landing a floor above, drew in her breath. She was certain that several suitors had gone way over the top in chat with Lady Alice, but 'honey' was not something you would associate with her abrasive, spiky daughter.

Lady Darriby-Jones thought this had gone on long enough. She resumed her descent, making sure to scrape her stout shoes against the stone steps.

"Ah, there you are, Mr Potters. It's so easy to get lost in this house. I see you've met my daughter, Lady Alice. Now, let me take you over to the west sitting room where your colleagues will be waiting for you. It's a veritable maze of a place, is it not?"

"Sure, thanks Lady Darriby, I'll just trot along behind ya, shall I? Bye, Lady A., no doubt I'll catch up later."

At ten minutes to twelve, Lady Darriby-Jones placed her secateurs in her wickerwork basket containing two-dozen cut roses and passed it to her maid, Lilly.

"Please take this to the garden room and arrange three vases for our American friends. One for each bedroom."

"Yes, milady." Lilly took the basket, turned away, remembered she was supposed to curtsy and did a strange spiral dipping motion as she swung her body round into position.

"If I live to a hundred, I don't think you'll get it right, Lilly."

"Yes milady, sorry milady."

Torino was waiting in the library, a few more bottles and decanters than normal on the low window ledge where the booze was kept; Lady Darriby-Jones always said it was the perfect height for little fingers, prompting Lord Darriby-Jones to suggest that they were unlikely to have any grandchildren at all as Lady Alice seemed wedded to her growing collection of horses. Alfie arrived a moment later, leading the three American workers in with him.

"Welcome to our home," Lady Darriby-Jones said, opening her arms as if she could wrap them around Darriby Hall. "I hope you'll be very happy here and achieve great things in the study of slugs. Now, where could my husband be?"

"Also, Mrs Hammerstein's not here," Alfie volunteered.

"Quite so. Where could she be?"

Torino coughed, the time-honoured way a servant, however senior, reacted to his or her employer.

"Yes, Torino?"

"I do believe Lord Darriby-Jones and Mrs Hammerstein were seen a few minutes ago on the south lawno."

"Lawno?"

"Torino means lawn, Professor Hammerstein." Lady Darriby-Jones turned to her butler and asked him to despatch someone instantly to collect the two delinquents and deliver them to the library.

A few minutes later, Torino opened the French windows leading onto the south lawn and the two missing persons entered the library.

"Ah dear, there you are," Lord Darriby-Jones said, as if he had been the one searching for her. "I must say, I'm sure I've seen Mrs Hammersmith..."

"Hammerstein," the professor corrected.

"Yes, quite, seen Mrs Hammerstein before somewhere. I'm just damned if I can recall the when and the where."

"Well, it's not in my time," Lady Darriby-Jones replied, "I never forget a face."

"As in coal face?" Mrs Hammerstein suddenly asked, then turned to explain to her colleagues. "Lady Darriby-Jones used to be Miss Jones, only daughter of Tobias Jones, the self-made coal magnate."

"True," Lady Darriby-Jones muttered, "now what about drinks? I for one am parched. What's your tipple, Mrs Hammerstein?"

"Well, I'm tempted by a pink gin." She watched as Torino made his silent way towards the drinks shelf. "Except I always say it's such a common drink. No, I'll have Scotch and water, please. A young person's drink, I always say."

These words hit Lady Darriby-Jones square in the chest, a sledge-hammer blow that knocked her backwards.

Why was this woman being so aggressive towards her? Maybe there was some past with Darriby that would need looking into.

The Mystery of the Obnoxious Englishwoman—but that lacked the appeal of the Mystery of the Polite Man. Perhaps the subject matter was a lot less savoury, too.

Torino did the necessary, supplying a variety of strange drinks including something called a 'Harvey Wallbanger,' which made Lady Darriby-Jones think of Darriby's nephew, Harvey Wallington, a twit of the first order but likeable all the same.

She was making a sacrifice for Darriby's sake, only she didn't quite know how much it would involve.

Chapter Three

Lady Darriby-Jones seldom lost her temper, or her patience, for that matter. Known throughout Oxfordshire and significant chunks of several surrounding counties, for her unflappable nature, she took great pride in dealing calmly and efficiently with whatever life sent her way.

Unless, as she discovered, that 'whatever' came in the form of one Mrs Albert Hammerstein.

"My husband believes he knows you, Mrs Hammerstein," she tried to make conversation on spotting her three seats away at the dining table that lunchtime.

"I expect he knows a number of attractive and sophisticated women," came the reply, no doubt suggesting, without saying, that Lady Darriby-Jones fitted neither category.

Well, she knew she wasn't sophisticated, not in the slightest, but she had hoped she might feature in the looks brigade, at least a bit. It irritated her intensely that Mrs

Hammerstein, who probably had a few years on her, had managed to position herself with the younger generation.

"Where were you before you met Professor Hammerstein?"

"Oh here and there," she said dismissively, then turned to address Alfie. "I say, Mr Burrows, what do young people do for fun around here? I know as a married lady, I have to be seen to be respectable, but I sure hanker after a bit of fun now and then. Why, it's as dead as a hibernating slug around here. Slugs do hibernate, don't they, dear?" She shouted this last question down one side of the long dining room table, stirring Major-General Fortescue-Brown sleeping gently next to her, slipping ever so steadily into the lap of the next person down the table, who happened to be Lady Alice, on time for lunch, for once.

"What? What's that, eh?"

Lady Darriby-Jones thought the old general might dive for cover and then start returning fire. Instead, he slipped back to the centre of whatever dream occupied his mind that day. She noted that Lady Alice dealt with the leaning general with surprising patience, propping him gently back to upright each time he slid over; certainly, far more patience than she ever showed for her family.

"If I've told you once, I've told you a million times, dear, most slugs don't hibernate in the winter. A few varieties do, for instance the..." The voice of Professor Hammerstein petered out as he realised no one was listening to him.

"I know what I'm gonna do," said Harrison Potters into the silence. "I'm going riding with this lovely sweet petal of a princess. She's only offered to take me out horseback riding all day tomorrow.

"What?"

That made Lady Darriby-Jones look up sharply; it was unlike Alfie Burrows to volunteer any conversation at lunch with company present, so even a 'what?' sounded alarm bells. She had put together the guest list at very short notice, falling back on the retired general and Miss Twittering, a spinster of similar age, as one did when pressed at eleven to provide guests for one o'clock sharp.

"Don't look at me like that, Mr Burrows, you've never shown the slightest interest in riding," Lady Alice added to the mix, her voice about eight-and-a-half out of ten for its cutting tone.

"It seems a merry band here today, Lady Darriby-Jones." Above all the normal whys and where-for-tos, Lady Darriby-Jones found herself wondering why this English appendix to the delightful American team was being so thoroughly obnoxious; almost as if she was on a mission to generate as much hatred as possible.

> *You'll go by the alias of Mrs Hammerstein. You're undercover but armed to the teeth. Just make sure you lob a few hand grenades in early on; that's bound to cause maximum confusion.*
>
> *"Yes sir, undercover, hand grenades, maximum confusion, got it, sir."*

Then she did get it, quite suddenly, in fact so suddenly that she had to pretend a coughing fit to hide her exuberance.

Mrs Hammerstein was no more married to Professor Hammerstein than she was.

And last time she checked, her matrimonial relationship was pointed towards Darriby, certainly not in Hammerstein's direction.

Something was up; this visit was some sort of sham. They were not lymacologists but imposters and she was right in the middle of a new adventure:

> *The Mystery of the Mysterious Americans*
> *Plus, One Obnoxious Englishwoman*

The key question that needed answering was why Mrs Hammerstein, or whatever her real name was, had to provoke a fight at every opportunity? She could understand friction between Alfie and Potters, the young American; they were, after all, fighting for 'possession' of Lady Alice. Fierce rivalry was to be expected in the Lady Alice quarter, but taking full broadsides from a professor's wife who had only been admitted on the promise of a square root of a slug whose Latin name had gone in one ear and straight out the other?

"Mrs Hammerstein, perhaps you would like to take a walk after lunch? I could show you the rose gardens, or even the maze that the gardeners are creating."

"I'd like to, Lady Darriby-Jones, except I doubt you could keep up with the rapid walk technique I learned in Seattle. I could get around your entire estate in less than an hour, leaving anyone accompanying me quite out of breath."

> *"I want maximum disruption to the natural rhythms of Darriby life," the briefing officer said. "You don't need to know why, just create havoc as rapidly as you can."*

Lady Darriby-Jones spent the rest of lunch thinking about decoys and smoke screens, despite Professor Hammerstein trying to strike up a fascinating discussion about the differences between British slugs and their American cousins.

Later that afternoon, Lady Darriby-Jones's suspicions were further raised when she heard a knock on the door of her private study.

"May I have a word, Lady Darriby-Jones?"

"Come in, Alfie." She normally had a rule that forbade others in her private study; servants, of course, but no residents or guests.

But, hang the rules, she smelt adventure in the air and loved the race it gave to her pulse.

"I wanted to ask your advice," he said, on being waved to a rather uncomfortable upright cane chair positioned in the bay window.

"Fire away, dear Alfie, fire away."

"It's just that I've spent the afternoon with Mr Potters, you know, the young American PhD student."

"The one that's taken a shine to Lady Alice?" That wasn't at all fair. She vowed to be kinder in the future.

"Precisely."

"How did you find him?"

"Well, that's the thing. I thought he would be a mine of knowledge about slugs, but…"

"He doesn't know the first thing."

"How did you know?" Alfie asked, visibly astounded by Lady Darriby-Jones's insight.

"Oh, just a hunch. Actually, I think the whole outfit is a sham. What did you think of Mrs Hammerstein?"

"Oh, her, rather outspoken, I suppose."

"Downright rude, I'd call it," Lady Darriby-Jones replied. "The whole bunch are suspect."

"Actually, not quite all," Alfie said, then explained that Professor Hammerstein certainly knew his slugs. "It's just the others I'm not so sure about. Righto, Lady Darriby-Jones, I need to be back in the thick of things. I officially only came out to collect these samples." Alfie proffered a box with a dozen or more little drawers in it.

"You mean you've brought a bunch of slugs into my private study? You better get them out quickly, young man, or you'll have me to answer to."

Alfie probably hadn't moved so fast since scrumping days as a kid. However, he did manage to back out, bowing every few steps and muttering an apology that Lady Darriby-Jones struggled to understand at all.

Torino met Alfie in the passageway outside. He carried a silver tray containing gin, a glass, and a bottle of angostura bitters.

"That will put her the right way," he said with a smile.

"Pardon, sir?" Torino could be more British than the British when he chose to lose his heavy Italian accent, usually when speaking to younger members of the wider Darriby entourage.

The Mystery of the American Slug

"Oh, I just said you carry that the right way."

"Thank you, sir."

"Think nothing of it."

"Is that you, Torino? I can hear everything you're saying because Alfie Burrows left the door wide open. Must have been born in a barn. I need a stiff pinkie after the day I've had."

"Coming up, Lady Darriby-Jones."

"Bring that boy back in with you, Torino."

"Yes, milady, coming in now."

"Here's the thing, Alfie dear. I'm thinking about you asking some pretty awful questions about slugs at dinner tonight. You see, I want you to expose Mr Potters as the non-slug expert he really is. Can you do that, now, Alfie?"

"Yes, Lady Darriby-Jones, if you will excuse me, I'll slip away now and compose a few penetrating questions for supper."

"Yes, away you go, my dear man. Preparation is everything, I always say."

Chapter Four

Both Lady Darriby-Jones and Mr Alfie Burrows were due to be disappointed that evening, at least in terms of exposing Harrison B. Potters for the fraud he was.

Their frustration didn't come about from the resilience of Potters under heavy questioning. Far from it.

The man just didn't show. And nor did Lady Alice. Lord Darriby-Jones didn't notice, but his secretary, Alfie Burrows, definitely did and barely a morsel passed his lips, although plenty of rich red wine did.

It wouldn't have mattered if Alfie had had the appetite of a whole rugger team; the food provided by the infamous Mrs Britain was inedible anyway, meaning not many morsels passed many lips that September evening.

Just as the meal was ending, however, the missing duo turned up, giggling and joking, swaying slightly as they walked down the lower gallery that ran at the back of the house from east wing to west wing. Lady Darriby-Jones was just leading the ladies of the party to the drawing room when she spotted the happy couple.

"So, who's this one, then?" Potters asked, looking at yet another portrait. All the men were in bright uniforms, the women in lavish dresses.

"That's great aunt Hilda," Lady Alice said after squinting at the picture for a moment. "No, I do believe it's my great grandmother."

"Wrong, Alice," Lady Darriby-Jones said, "it's your namesake."

"Oh, Mr Potters," Lady Alice suddenly grew serious, "may I have the honour of presenting Lady Darriby, otherwise known by the delightful name of Alice Morton Catherine Dorothy Darriby, the exact same names as me!"

"Except, my dear, you have the added name of Jones. Darriby-Jones is your surname."

"Yes, mother, quite right. Mr Potters, this lovely lady is none other than my grandmother, the mother of Papa, although I never knew her. I'm told that we share certain attributes. She died shortly after Papa and Mother married."

"How far back do all these paintings go?"

"Oh, I don't know, but they're all in date order. Do you want to go all the way to the east wing to see where it all starts? It might be fun to trace the Darriby line back through the ages to the first ever Darriby. Actually, coming to think of it, you can't have a first Darriby; it's a little like chicken and egg, isn't it?"

The Mystery of the American Slug

"I think an early bed might be called for, Alice," her mother said, a little bit affronted; well, who wouldn't be when your only daughter was half-cut and deciding to spend the evening with a total fraud, could be a scam artist, one of the best, most likely. Perhaps the little horror had worn his home patch incredibly thin so had made his way across the pond to try his luck with the English.

Whatever this despicable man was, he could not claim to be a doctorate student engrossed in the life-mating patterns of slugs.

So why was he here, together with the little American entourage?

And why was Mrs Hammerstein so abrasive, especially with her?

Surprisingly, Lady Alice did as bid and said a rather shaky goodnight to all of them in the gallery, repeating the process more than once, before wobbling off in the general direction of her bedroom.

"What's been going on, Mr Potters?" Lady Darriby-Jones asked when Alice eventually made it safely out of earshot.

"Oh, a man's gotta have some fun from time to time, don't grind down on the poor lad," Mrs Hammerstein cried. The way she said, 'poor lad' clicked with Lady Darriby-Jones.

"Birmingham," she uttered under her breath.

"What did you say?" Mrs Hammerstein's words were a little too sharp.

"He's a very nice man," Lady Darriby-Jones replied, secretly delighted with the quick wit of her answer. No need in letting suspect number two know that you were making rapid tracks her way.

Then Betty Bollinger made her move upon the board.

"You mustn't worry about Mr Potters, Lady Darriby-Jones. He's a little worse for wear at the moment. Perhaps I can lead him away someplace and let him sober up."

"I think Bedfordshire, perhaps?"

"Oh, is that nearby? We rather hoped to stay here for the duration, Lady Darriby-Jones."

By the time, Lady Darriby-Jones had explained that Bedfordshire was both a county in England, actually reasonably close to them, and a euphemism for calling it a day and popping off to lay your head down for some kip, she was quite exhausted herself; with the tension of the aggressive, so called, 'Mrs Hammerstein' forever present, it was hardly surprising.

After another flurry of goodnight calls, some sincere, some distinctly not so, they all climbed the stairs to their respective Bedfordshires, knowing the menfolk would be not long behind them; lymacology is, after all, a demanding subject and takes its toll on both mind and body.

The shot pierced through the slumbering bliss of Darriby Hall. Then, as suddenly as it happened, it was gone again, as happens with guns, letting Darriby Hall settle back into quietness. Lady Darriby-Jones thought it a part of her

The Mystery of the American Slug

dream. She opened her eyes, felt obliged to look up and check on Darriby, snoring contentedly beside her. No problems there. Maybe it had been a dream, she thought, as she sunk back down on the pillows.

But it was too piercing, too lifelike to be a dream; it was there as a splintering crack, then gone again. She would have to go and investigate. She rose from her bed, found her dressing gown and slipped it on, fumbling with the tie and then stumbling over something as she searched for her slippers.

"Blow!" she said as she went down on all fours, a pile of books scattering around her. She didn't bother with the titles; they were Darriby's side of the bed, hence would be slug-orientated. The dear man didn't read anything else. Not that she could be considered a wide reader. Her interest in literature was confined to crime novels, particularly murder mysteries where she could piece together the clues and arrive at the murderer a split second before the hero.

That made her the hero of everything she read, yet she never seemed to get any recognition for it.

She looked back, Darriby still snoring, dear man and all that. But she had a mission to undertake. She found her missing slipper through a process of elimination, working backwards from when she last wore it the night before. It had to be under the bed; her mind was working clearly. Darriby would have kicked it under the bed when he climbed in last night.

Her mind was always top-notch in the early morning. Exiting the bedroom, she glanced at the clock.

It was twelve minutes to five. In twelve minutes' time, the early brigade of the staff would be stumbling from their bedrooms to light stoves, fetch coal and boil water. The noise was in the past, hence unlikely to be a servant knocking something over; she had yet to meet a servant of any description who would gladly rise twenty-odd minutes before the prescribed time.

So, if not the staff, it must be either family or guests. Being a mother, she went first to Lady Alice's room, trying to open the door without disturbing her.

"Hello, mother, did you hear that noise also?" Lady Alice was four minutes behind her mother, still fumbling for her slippers.

"Yes, what was it?"

"A gun," she said, sure as anything.

"Not a..."

"No, not one of Papa's shotguns, more a handgun. I woke with a sore head, was getting some water from the bathroom. Mother, it came from in there."

"In where, darling?" With no light, except a dim one on the landing, Lady Alice's indicative movements were useless.

"In the American quarters, mother, where else?"

She had a point, Lady Darriby-Jones considered. Where else could it come from? Only herself, and she would hardly seek the sound's source if she were the instigator.

"We'd better rouse them," she said. "Get dressed and come to the library. I'll bang on the door now to wake them, then get dressed myself. Everyone in the library in five minutes."

The Mystery of the American Slug

"It's going to take you forever to wake Papa," Lady Alice replied. "You go back and get him ready. I'll bang on the door. Gosh, what a palaver."

Five minutes proved hopelessly unrealistic; fifteen saw some people located in the library, Lord and Lady Darriby-Jones amongst them, a hastily dressed Torino also.

"Go and get everyone in here, Torino," Lady Darriby-Jones said, "we need the whole household from boot-boy upwards."

Over the following fifteen minutes, the library started to fill up, many shy young servants who would normally spend their days in the pantries and laundry rooms and rarely, if ever, surface on the main floor.

"Torino, please count all staff members. I'll do the same for guests and family."

"Yes, milady." Torino commanded considerable authority below stairs and Lady Darriby-Jones noted them forming up in the position they obviously took to eat their meals; that made imminent sense, and she applied the same structure to the upstairs contingent. Yet, try as she might, Lady Darriby-Jones could not remember who had sat where the night before. To make matters worse, hers was an infinitely simpler job than Torino's; just Lord Baritone, forgiven after repairing the ancient Darriby Duck, Professor Plumer, still talking slugs at the top of his voice, the four Americans and the three family members. Oh, and Alfie, of course, sitting right in the corner, easily forgotten.

Yet, they were short two people.

Lady Alice and Harrison B. Potters.

"Where's Lady Alice?" Alfie sprang to his feet after reaching the same realisation as Lady Darriby-Jones, panicking at the thought of losing the love of his life, albeit love kept at a distinct distance.

"Here I am, silly." She entered the library, looking ready for a show jumping event; perfect jodhpurs, riding hat set back on her head to reveal her disdain to everyone who dared to look, even a whip which she looked quite capable of using. "I went to check the horses."

"Thank goodness," he replied, "I thought for a moment that…"

"No, don't be a silly, silly. Mother could have told you I'm alright; she saw me only a few minutes ago."

"More like half-an-hour, dear," Lady Darriby-Jones replied, "but where the devil is Mr Potters?"

Nobody had seen Mr Potters since his rather drunken retreat to bed the night before. Probably sleeping off an almighty hangover.

Lady Darriby-Jones had to amend her thought ten minutes later when the search for Potters took them up to his bedroom where he lay dead on the bed, blood pooling on the antique Persian rug on the floor; someone had definitely seen Potters since then, because someone had taken aim and shot him as he slept, presumably heavily after the alcohol he had consumed with Lady Alice the day before.

He would seem to be suffering from the hangover to cure all hangovers.

Chapter Five

"It's a beauty of a shot," Baritone said, "straight through the heart. I think the rug's seen better days, though."

Lady Darriby-Jones stepped back from the bedside and saw the blood-stained rug.

"That wasn't...?" she almost dared not ask.

"It is, Mother," confirmed Lady Alice with the detachment from all emotion she was famous for, "won't get ten bob for that now."

Lady Darriby-Jones tried to remember which Darriby ancestor had paid a small fortune for that rug when coming back from his grand tour.

"What about poor Mr Potters?" came a wail from the back of the crowd assembled around the bed, as if the smell of blood had caused a flock of vultures to land by the fresh carcass. Everyone turned to see Betty Bollinger looking distraught. She looked at those staring at her for a moment and something caught fire inside. "The poor man meant nothing to y'all. How can you be lacking in emotion so much? You care more about a stupid rug than the fact a man has been murdered?" Tears flowed down her face. Alfie jumped out of a corner and pulled his handkerchief from his pocket, holding it out in front of her, creating a tiny element of decency in an indecent world.

"It's not..." started Lady Darriby-Jones, but then stopped, thinking it not worth making excuses.

They had put a rug ahead of a man's life.

Or rather his death, the end of life.

"We need to call the police. Torino, please send someone to run down to the village for the police station."

"No need, milady."

"What?"

"We have telefono, milady."

"Yes, yes, of course." She returned her gaze to the dead body lying peacefully on the bed, mid-yawn by the look of things. What should she do before the police arrived? Would it be the familiar and genial Sergeant 'Haddock' Fisher or the abrasive and hopelessly self-important DCI 'Rude' Manners?

She thought it unlikely for Manners to pass up an opportunity like this.

"Right," she said, turning to face the crowd in the room, "first things first." She searched the sea of faces for somebody with authority. "Ah, Lord Baritone, could you please get everyone back down to the library? It's important not to disturb things up here and I'm sure the police will want a chat with everyone in their attempts to ascertain what has happened to poor Mr Potters."

Lord Baritone rose to the task, ushering and ordering like a sergeant-major; perhaps, Lady Darriby-Jones mused, the man had missed his calling. That was a problem with the aristocracy she had married into; there was no correlation between ability and opportunity. Baritone would make a perfect non-commissioned officer but a dreadful general.

Perhaps, she wondered, if a few more men like her father had been in charge during the last war...but this was getting her nowhere.

"Alfie and Alice, stay a moment. I want to consult with you." This gave Alfie a reprieve from the heavy-handed tactics of Baritone who took delight in marshalling a rival for Alice out of the room. He grunted his disapproval and added an extra layer of vigour to his attempt to rid the room of all others, including clipping the ear of a boot boy who stood, mouth wide open, staring at the corpse on the bed.

Baritone, in fact, hung back when the room was cleared, obviously hoping to be a part of Lady Darriby-Jones's inner circle, or else just not wanting anybody close to Lady Alice, who he, apparently, still had not given up on.

"Please make sure they all get to the library, Barry." His look of annoyance stayed with Lady Darriby-Jones when Alfie closed the bedroom door on him. She would not have him staying at Darriby Hall at all, except that he had become a favourite of her husband after forking out to have Darriby Duck repaired by expert stonemasons.

Then there was the strange crucible or casket stuffed inside the duck, sitting right where she imagined a duck's heart would be. Nobody could open it, not even the village blacksmith who had started a neat side line in servicing motor cars and selling petrol.

But why was she puzzling about a trivial thing like that when she had a murder on her hands?

And a murderer in their midst.

"Take note of everything, you two," she said, returning her own concentration to the murder scene before them, "look for anything unusual or unexpected, note how the body lies and..."

"Like clues, you mean, Mother?"

"Yes, I rather think I do."

They had ten minutes to inspect the crime scene before the jangling and whining of police sirens came up the drive. Another three minutes and Torino opened the door, stepped back and DCI Manners burst into the room.

"What are you doing?" he cried angrily. "You can't go snooping about here. I need to look for clues. PC Miller, escort these three amateur, would-be sleuths out of the room."

"Where shall I take them, sir?"

"Anywhere you damned well please, just not contaminating my crime scene. Ah, what's this?" He kicked at the rug and bent to wipe blood off his shoes, using a corner of the sheet that lay hanging close to the floor. "Blasted blood!" The whole sheet slipped off the bed and the others in the room, Lady Darriby-Jones included, watched as the red blood spread steadily across the white sheet, like the tide coming in.

"You still here?" he snarled, as physics worked on the dead body and it left the position of death and slipped onto the floor, lying neatly on the rug, as if it had been put there deliberately as a way of dragging the corpse away.

"We're just going, DCI Manners," Lady Alice said with a perfect amount of haughtiness, producing mutterings of 'bloody aristos, think they own the place' as they closed the door on the scene.

"As a matter of fact, you do," Alfie said with the door closed as they made their way down the passage and across the gallery towards the main staircase.

"Do what?" Lady Darriby-Jones asked.

"Own the place."

To which answer, Lady Alice threw back her head and laughed out loud, drowning the quiet, fearful atmosphere of the Darriby Hall murder scene in raucous laughter.

"Alfie, you're quite the wit," she said.

"Thanks, Lady Alice. You're not too bad yourself when you get going." It was a trivial answer, quickly forgotten, but her words stayed with Alfie long afterwards, eating their way into his consciousness.

It was only much later that day that it came to him. Lady Alice had called him 'Alfie' for the first time. Prior to that, it had always been 'Mr Burrows'.

Things were looking up. Not for poor Potters, but certainly for young Alfie.

Lady Darriby-Jones stood before a crowd in the library, trying to work out the general atmosphere from all the faces she knew.

Expectation.

That's what it was. Lord Darriby-Jones, the other main contender for the leadership role, had lost himself in deep discussion with Sir John Plumer and Professor Hammerstein, forming a trio of slug experts and effectively cutting them off from the real world. That left her to take charge.

"Right everybody," she started, actually having no idea what she was going to say, "no, quiet at the back, young David, there's only room for one person at a time to talk and whether you like it or not, that's going to be me." David Jones was a young footman who had a sort of claim on kinship with Lady Darriby-Jones. There was little substance to it, Jones being a common enough name in her native Wales. But his father had died in a terrible mining disaster back at the turn of the century and just before the lad's birth. He had worked in another mine, one ran much more with an eye to a quick profit than those under the control of 'Old Jonesy'. The boy's mother had developed a fear of her only child going down the mines and Lady Darriby-Jones, newly married, had offered the boy a place at Darriby when the lad became of working age. She had completely forgotten about it until 1919, when the youngster had turned up with a letter in his pocket from his mother.

He had proved to be a good worker, if something of a gossip, a good gossip being something the south Welsh miners delighted in.

But now, for once, he fell silent.

"I think it would be a good idea to build up a picture of everybody's whereabouts and observations over the last twelve hours. Torino, could you please manage the staff, while Lord Baritone and I lead the way with family and guests." She felt a need to include Barry Baritone in something more than herding people towards a waiting pen.

"Of course, milady," Torino replied, "I will set about this immediately."

"Okey, dokey," said Baritone, "whose first for a good grilling?"

Chapter Six

"Coffee, milady?" Torino asked, thirty minutes into the questioning, in which much larking about and increasingly bawdy humour was evident at the other end of the library where the staff had settled. Or, at least, the older ones had settled while the younger generation messed about, their voices ever louder.

"Yes, lovely," she replied. "I tell you what, Torino. Release two of the kitchen staff and make it coffee and sandwiches for everyone."

"In the library, milady?"

"Yes, right here in the library. Everyone can eat here. If there aren't enough chairs and tables, they can eat with plates off their laps, like a picnic. I know it's not the done thing, but we're living through unusual times, Torino. I'm sure everybody's tummy is rumbling with equal rumbuctioness." She thought that probably wasn't a word the dictionary would recognise but it seemed to suit the occasion. "Oh, and don't select Mrs Britain; we don't want more untimely deaths on our hands!"

As coffee and sandwiches were served–smoked salmon for the family and guests, cheese and homemade pickle for the rest–Lady Darriby-Jones took stock.

She had interviewed the Americans first, thinking them most likely to have noticed something out of the ordinary, but had drawn stumps with that particular line of enquiry. She would go through the form with Darriby, her husband, but there seemed little point; he was perpetually in a world of his own, only occasionally surfacing to make the odd comment; how could someone be so engrossed in one subject that everything else passed him by. Sometimes, she hankered after a life in which her husband collected stamps or coins; even prize bulls would be better than slugs.

Her thoughts returned to the pointlessness of interviewing her husband. He had been snoring noisily when the shot rang out to split the morning apart. She was a witness to his innocence.

Then she thought that with him being fast asleep, she couldn't claim him as a witness; she was every bit in the frame as the next one in line.

On first hearing the shot, she had considered it might be a car backfiring or a poacher out doing his business, but the neat exit wound and the lodged bullet anchoring the expensive rug to the floor told a different story.

They had a mystery but any one of fifty occupants of the house that night could have done it, her included, although that was preposterous because she would have known if it had been her.

The Mystery of the American Slug

She briefly considered the possibility of a sleepwalker, maybe even herself, but dismissed it on the basis that that sort of palaver only happened in cheap novels. This was a first-class mystery, not some run-down puzzle that you could squeeze into a Christmas cracker.

Somehow, she had to narrow down the suspect list; it being impossible to question fifty suspects thoroughly. Well, maybe the police could do that by drafting in extra detectives but she was one person, although she felt sure she could rely on assistance from Alfie and Baritone, possibly Alice if she got off her high horse, literally, for one single moment.

Thinking of the police led her to consider what Manners was up to. Other than dismissing everyone from the bedroom upstairs, a process already started by her, they hadn't heard a word from any officer of the law since they arrived over an hour ago. Surely, they would want to talk to everybody involved, however on-the-fringe that involvement might have been.

Well, she would continue investing her time in the close questioning the boys in blue should have been doing; if it happened to produce a result, so be it. Her blood quickened as she thought about Frank Hoosish and the devilry he was driven to by misdirected rage. It made her wonder how many murders were committed through miscommunication rather than perfect clarity of thought and action; those were the particularly sinister ones.

But then, would poor Potters have cared too much as to the reasons for his sudden death? It was an absolute; a person was alive or dead, just like you were either born Welsh or you weren't.

Maybe, just maybe, this one filled the 'oh I shot you by mistake but never mind' slot also. That meant they had to look beyond the obvious.

Trust No One and Question Everything

She would have liked that as the Darriby-Jones motto, instead of some Latin dribble she never could remember and seemed to translate a little differently every time.

Back to the questioning then. She would do Sir John Plumer and then Baritone, Alice and Alfie, to finish off. She glanced at Torino, wondering how he was getting on. He looked up at that moment, over the head of a young girl, Sally, or maybe Sarah, Lady Darriby-Jones didn't recall, but saw a frustrated look on Torino's face; he too was getting nowhere.

"Sir John, might I ask you to come upstairs a moment? Just a few questions to see if you recall anything of interest." Upstairs meant the higher layers of shelves, reached by a set of sliding stairs resting on a metal frame that circled the huge library. The viewing platform widened at one point, allowing enough space for a desk and chair plus two old leather armchairs.

Lady Darriby-Jones wasn't much of a reader, but if she had been, this is where she would choose to indulge her passion. Her interest in the library was more the window seat-turned-drinks collection on the ground floor; but even in exceptional circumstances such as 'The Shoot-out at Darriby Corral', it was a little early for the pink gin she felt sure her doctor would prescribe.

She had just settled into a comfortably ancient armchair, Sir John Plumer facing her, when Torino gave a great and excited cry from below.

"Here, we have a clue, Lady Darriby-Jones. Oh, where is milady?"

"Up here, Torino."

"Coming milady." And the usual slow glide was replaced with a tumultuous rush as he made his way up to her, dragging the young scullery maid behind him.

"A clue, milady." He turned to the young girl and said, "Sally, tell milady what you said to me."

"Well, milady, it was like this. You see, I heard the shot like anybody else, didn't I?"

Lady Darriby-Jones wondered whether she expected an answer to this question, but the girl was moving on too fast.

"It made me proper frightened, didn't it?"

How do you speak in constant question mode, Lady Darriby-Jones thought; they should be statements of facts, not seeking confirmation from her audience. This approach would never do in a court of law. She had seen a clever play set in a courtroom once; the details of the plot evaded her, but she remembered the great emphasis they placed on correct procedure. They would make mincemeat of young Sally.

"A moment later, I sees a figure running through them rodo-things, you know, milady, them bushes that have the pretty flowers."

"Well done, Sally. This could be a vital clue, helping us determine who the murderer is."

"Thank you, milady."

"And the bushes are rhododendrons. Don't ask me how to spell it but try practicing it before you go to bed at night."

"Yes, milady. Thank you, milady." A curtsy and Sally was gone, Torino escorting her back down the moving staircase, a first for young Sally who harboured a sudden ambition to graduate up to housemaid from scullery maid and dust these wonderful shelves all day long. The thought made her smile broadly.

Lady Darriby-Jones smiled just as widely because the information Sally had given was a clue–or rather, a lead. Now they were really going places.

Chapter Seven

"How much longer are we going to be stuck here?" Mrs Hammerstein wanted to know, not that she had anywhere in particular to go to. She had a golden globe in her hand which she chucked in the air and caught in her other hand, before repeating the process, like slow-motion juggling with one ball; elementary stuff but she kept missing the catch, particularly with her left hand, so it banged on the table and rolled a short distance with whatever force or energy it still had after the impact.

"I think the general picture is we're gonna be here until the cops sort themselves out," her husband replied, clearly annoyed about the interruption dragging him away from slug-talk. "Now will you please stop playing with that damned croquet ball."

"It ain't no croquet ball, mister," she replied, putting on a mock American accent that could have come from the music hall comedy night.

Lady Darriby-Jones sighed as she descended the steps.

"It might be an idea, Mrs Hammerstein, not to throw it about too much as it's probably of significant value." She actually had no idea as to valuation, just knowing that it was shiny and looked the part; it could be tin underneath for all she knew.

"Here, you have it." She chucked it straight at Lady Darriby-Jones, only her aim was not too hot. It hit Mr Hammerstein on the shoulder with a cracking-sound, and fell to the floor, just as Lady Darriby-Jones arrived at the bottom of the steps. Mr Hammerstein reacted as if a fly had buzzed by, just an irritated swipe following a quick look.

Lady Darriby-Jones, however, bent at the waist and picked up the object.

"It's cracked open," she said. "We've been trying to get it open since Lord Baritone brought it back last week. What's this?"

But nobody was paying her any attention. The door to the library had opened and DCI Manners stood in the doorway, surveying the scene laid out before him.

"What's this?" he said.

"What's what?" Lady Darriby-Jones was too absorbed in the golden globe, casket or ball, whatever it was.

"Why are all these people here? Does it make sense with words of one syllable?"

"Actually, sir, people has two syllables, just for the record, sir." Sergeant Fisher was a brave man to correct his boss in public, or probably just fed up with him and counting the days to retirement.

"Hold your tongue, Fisher, unless you want to face demotion to PC for the last few years of your service."

"Sorry sir."

"These people, Mr Manners, are here waiting for your officers to conduct interviews. They've been waiting patiently since you arrived." Lady Darriby-Jones could put ice into her words when she so chose.

"Send them away. We don't need to conduct pointless interviews when everybody fibs to death, anyway. We're going to rely on science to sort this case out. We've sent the slug to ballistics and the body to forensics. That way we get solid answers to all the questions instead of airy-fairy stuff we can't rely on."

With the best part of fifty people in a room, you're never going to get total silence, not while they're breathing at any rate. But the library of Darriby Hall was as close to it as you're ever going to get. The normal hum of laughter, complaint and general movement came to a sudden stop when DCI 'Rude' Manners let forth. It took Lady Darriby-Jones to release the tension that promised to burst the library apart.

"Alright, we've had a difficult morning everybody, but now we've got to get about our business and pretend this is just another day." She was thinking routine was a great thing, a salve to anger, but she needed something else; then it came to her. "As soon as we've solved this murder, there's going to be a half-day holiday for everyone."

That got a ragged cheer from the staff and the situation was diffused like smoke disappearing into the sky.

A few minutes later, a convoy of police cars took off down the drive and Darriby Hall could almost get back to normal.

Except for a dead American.

And a broken gold casket with the piece of paper that Lady Darriby-Jones had picked up and secreted in the pocket of her skirt.

"Take a look at this," Lady Darriby-Jones said to Alfie and Lady Alice the moment they had settled into drinks in a now deserted library, instructions for cold meat and salad for lunch sent off with Torino.

"What on earth is it?" Lady Alice took it from her mother and squinted at it.

"I've no idea. It's in a foreign language and it's not Welsh, that's for sure."

"I think it's English," Alfie said when his turn came to look at it. "It's just handwritten and very old. You see how the letters are so hard to make out? But it seems to be some form of a legal document from ages ago."

"Well, it's another mystery altogether," said Lady Alice. "It can't have anything to do with poor Harrison murdered in his bed."

"No, I don't think there can be a connection. I'll send it to our lawyers when we get a chance. Right now, I need a refill. Will you do the honours, Alfie? I don't want to disturb Torino when he's running about trying to restore order downstairs."

"It will be my pleasure, Lady Darriby-Jones," Alfie replied, thinking it must be possible to replicate that particular shade of pink, not wanting his ignorance displayed in front of Lady Alice.

Two days passed with no word from anyone in the police. It started to seem that it had all been a bad dream, except that there was an obvious gap in the American contingent. Mrs Hammerstein had changed, however. Some of the abrasiveness had dropped away, as if it had all been an act in the first place. She wasn't friendly or approachable, just that the barbs were lacking, no barrage of spiteful remarks issuing forth, or whatever spiteful remarks do.

Then, on the Wednesday, around about half-past-three, the same convoy tracked its way back up the drive, coming to a choreographed halt in a semi-circle on the drive. DCI Manners always insisted on coming in the front door, despite the fact that it stuck terribly. To be fair, Torino didn't try that hard to drag it open and Lady Darriby-Jones found herself battling against her laughter, trying valiantly to bury it deep within her chest.

"Welcome DIC Manners," Torino said when he eventually got the door open.

"It's DCI."

"Pardon?"

"Oh, never mind. I want everyone in the library immediately."

It so happened that the lymacologists, with Alfie in attendance and taking notes, were away on the far side of the immediate grounds, quite close to the dower house.

Young Jones was sent to fetch them. He explained afterwards how he hadn't been able to find them despite searching for ever, then had bumped into Alfie just as he made his dejected way back to Darriby Hall. Alfie led him to the others, who refused to come until an important experiment had been completed.

Thus, it was much closer to five in the afternoon when the whole household finally managed to gather in the library as instructed by Manners almost ninety minutes earlier.

"Right, the ballistics report came in. They rushed it through for me. It makes for an interesting read." He patted his jacket pocket, obviously enjoying not showing the report to anyone else. "It says the bullet was fired by a Colt M1911. That just so happens to be an American made pistol not seen much over here. I propose now to search the rooms all these Americans have been staying in without any of you leaving this room. What?" Sergeant Fisher had lent over and whispered something in his ear. "Speak up, man, I'm not a bat."

"Sir, it would be advisable to have a representative of the house with us as we search. That way, we can't be accused of planting anything."

"I would never..."

"I know, sir, but we have to be careful. People can get up to all kinds of tricks."

"Very well. Lady Darriby-Jones can come upstairs with you and me, Fisher, while the others in my team stay down here and ensure nobody leaves. That way, our murderer can't make a mad dash for freedom."

Lady Darriby-Jones was sure that Sergeant Fisher winked at her as he held the door open for his boss and her.

They had searched Potters' room already, so the DCI went straight to Betty Bollinger's and took apparent delight in reducing the neat bedroom to its component parts and then leaving them there.

"Nothing here, sir." They moved to the Hammerstein's room where Lady Darriby-Jones noted something strange immediately.

"Separate beds," she said, "these beds were always pushed together, but now they're fully apart."

"So what?" Manners said belligerently, "lots of people sleep apart. I hear the King does."

"Yes, I believe he does," she replied.

"Oh, so we're in with royalty now, are we?"

"I know a few ladies-in-waiting."

Nothing, either, in the Hammerstein's room, at least no gun. Manners searched the tiny desk, scattering papers onto the floor in his evident frustration. "No gun anywhere," he said, sounding like a spoilt child denied an ice cream on a Sunday outing.

Lady Darriby-Jones turned to leave the room. Then her keen eyes spotted some interesting papers lying on the floor where Manners had scattered them. From a distance of ten feet, they looked identical to the single page discovered when the golden globe had broken.

Somewhere, in some distant part of her mind, a little piece of the jigsaw puzzle fitted into place. She didn't say anything because to have done so would have invited ridicule. She was pretty immune to Manners' crude sarcasm, being too literal to really understand it, but didn't point out the connection between the papers in the Hammerstein's bedroom and the one in her skirt pocket, because she didn't want an obnoxious policeman messing everything up with his clumsy actions and accusations.

Besides, she needed time to think. And where better to go for a think than the spacious grounds of Darriby Hall.

Chapter Eight

"Well," said DCI Manners on the telephone, Lady Darriby-Jones's telephone to be precise, "the next thing I'm going to do is follow up the lead I got from questioning every member of the household, top down. That's the sighting of the person or suspect, sir, fleeing from the bushes a few moments after the shot was heard. Yes sir, I should have a result for you by tomorrow. That's very kind of you, sir. I shall look forward to it."

"'His lead' and 'his questioning', the cheek of it," Lady Darriby-Jones added when reciting the substance of Manners' phone call to his superior in Oxford when she was returned to the library, bedroom search over. All of them were told to stay put until further instructions, an order given with embarrassment by Sergeant Fisher, who knew a big house like Darriby Hall didn't run itself. To Lady Darriby-Jones's credit, she hadn't broadcasted her indignation to the wider audience but, instead, had pulled Alfie and Lady Alice aside.

"It's incredibly stupid of the man to speak of results tomorrow when he hasn't got a clue," Lady Alice said.

"Yes, but he will find some reason why it's somebody else's fault come tomorrow," Lady Darriby-Jones replied, "and I'm in the front line for the blame game. No doubt one part of his mind is working away on the excuses even now."

To make matters worse, Manners, who had accompanied Lady Darriby-Jones back to the library, now addressed the wider Darriby community, somewhat pompously telling everyone that the police were close to finding the murderer and they were all to sit tight for a little longer.

"Police state," someone called from the dim recesses where the private study cubicles were.

"Take that man's name, sergeant," Manners snapped, as if still in the army during the war. He had spent the first few weeks in the most miserable conditions on the front line, then the rest of the war training new Military Police recruits in considerable comfort in a country home not unlike Darriby Hall, gaining a distinct dislike of the aristocracy in the process. The scariest moment came with the prospect of a parachute jump; however, Manners managed to break his leg the day before during a football match between the army and the remaining staff. By the time the plaster came off, they had scrapped that part of the training for the very good reason that it was highly unlikely that a military policeman would ever need to use a parachute when the pilots weren't even issued with them.

"Now, where's the filly called Sally?"

"Over here, sir," came the smallest of voices.

"Got a room where me and Sergeant Fisher can interview her?"

"Better than that," replied Lady Darriby-Jones, wanting to avoid putting Sally through the 'Manners Mill' if she could possibly avoid it, "we have her statement already prepared, DCI Manners. Mr Burrows typed it up the other day."

"No, we have to do it the proper way, can't be relying on amateurs. Where would the world be if amateurs ran the things that really matter? Would you go to an amateur doctor if you broke your leg? No, I thought not." He tapped his leg as he spoke, memories of the three years he spent in the army flooding back; particularly the disdain with which he was held as a temporary lieutenant by the Earl of Sandham's family.

"You can use the small dining room. Sally will know where it is. Can I dismiss everyone now, DCI Manners?"

"And give the murderer free rein to escape? Are you daft, woman?" He turned to his sergeant and ordered him to bring young Sally along immediately.

"Sir, there's a problem."

"Not another one, sergeant. What now?"

"Well, if this is Sally Skinner we're talking about," he looked over his glasses before continuing, "yes, I see it is. She's only fifteen, sir."

"So? Does she speak English? Does she have a brain in her head? Well, then we'll go ahead."

"Sir, the problem is one of admissibility in court." Actually, Sergeant 'Haddock' Fisher had no idea whether this would be an issue or even have any relevance in court, if it ever got that far. But he did know that no way this side of the underworld was he going to lead Sally Skinner into the tender mercies of DCI 'Rude' Manners without a barrage of support. And, he knew who he wanted for that barrage.

"Sir, the best way around this is to have an independent adult with her, someone preferably with credibility, sir."

"That rules out anyone I can see, Fisher." He chortled at his own joke, with Fisher hoping for a little less chortling and a bit more choking, but not to be. Eventually, he agreed to Lady Darriby-Jones accompanying Sally Skinner during the interrogation planned for the small dining room.

Six minutes later, barely into the interview, Lady Darriby-Jones asked for a pause and led Manners out into the pantry that served the small dining room.

"Mr Manners, you can't treat people in this way."

"What way?" But he knew, he just wanted to make Lady Darriby-Jones say it.

So she did.

"You can't treat a young girl with such aggression. You need to calm down, Mr Manners. Besides, you won't get anything from her with your attitude. Let me show you how to get the most out of Sally."

"I can't."

"Why not?" But then she realised. "You know, we don't need Sergeant Fisher in there if you'd be more comfortable on your own."

They went back in, roles reversed in that Manners did the observing while Lady Darriby-Jones asked the questions. They ended up after thirty minutes with a perfectly acceptable statement and a smiling Sally who was given the rest of the day off.

"That's how you do it, Mr Manners," she wanted to say but didn't. Men have their pride and Lady Darriby-Jones had learnt over the years how to extract the most from the situation without running rampant over that particular emotion.

"Who do you think did it, Mr Manners?" she had asked when Fisher had been called back in to escort Sally to wherever she went on her time off. Manners seemed to have forgotten his instruction for everyone to stay in the library and she hoped that meant no further restrictions. The sooner she got them all back to a regular routine, the better.

"I dunno," he admitted, for once being frank with her, "could be you for all I know."

"It wasn't me," she replied, her patience somewhat strained. Besides, it was close to pink gin time. "You know you can interview me, if you like."

"No, couldn't be bothered. Besides, it's almost me tea time. Pork steak tonight. Pork steak and apple pie."

"Well, you run off then, Mr Manners. I've got a load of personal stuff to do as well."

Tracking down a murderer was deeply personal. After all, what else would she do with her time?

"Baritone, I have need of your particular skill set." Lady Darriby-Jones had to dance carefully around Barry Baritone. He wasn't exactly best pleased with her and only hung around because he had hopes for Alice and him. Yet, there was a half-decent side to him, it's just that it was buried deep within the aggression and barely ever surfaced.

"Yes, Lady Darriby-Jones?"

"I want to search the Americans in person and believe you are best equipped to do so. Do you agree?"

"I certainly do. Leave it all to me."

"Only remember, they're our friends. I mean don't go too roughly on them." She knew Baritone well. It was a risk using him, but she wanted to stay distant from the search. The objective of remaining aloof from the search sent her upstairs to the library, back to where the two old armchairs were. Of course, she picked the one with the best view of the library floor below her.

It took eighteen seconds to find the gun. Another ten seconds to listen to the garbled statement of surprise and innocence and then it became decision time.

Chapter Nine

Well, Lady Darriby-Jones had assumed it was decision time, but when the library door banged open and the police filed in, she lost both her concentration and her decisiveness. That's principally because the boys in blue came straight for her and that didn't make for too pleasant an occurrence.

"Lady Darriby-Jones," Manners started, puffing a bit from climbing the stairs to the upper level of the library, "you're under..."

He got no further than that. Still, it was the closest thing to being collared that Lady Darriby-Jones had ever experienced. The next in line in terms of nearly-nicked was as a seventeen-year-old when she had ridden her bicycle the wrong way down a one-way street. The local copper at the time hated kids, particularly those whose parents were rich enough to get one of the new safety bicycles with the revolutionary Dunlop pneumatic tyres. She had received a royal telling off and ended up walking home with tears in her eyes while the policeman rode home in style on her bike.

The next day, that same policeman and his sergeant were paid a visit by a very cross mine owner and father. She would never forget the feeling of intense embarrassment as the plod was forced to apologise to her when he brought her bicycle back, newly cleaned and polished by the plod in question.

Manners got no further for the simple reason that his attempt to place Lady Darriby-Jones under arrest was shouted down instantly, demonstrating that the power of the police came to nothing much when pitted against the mob's overwhelming strength.

"Well, who then?" Manners cried at one point in typical Pontius Pilate mode.

"Isn't that for you to decide based on the evidence rather than gut instinct?" Lady Darriby-Jones replied, her voice lost to the volume of the crowd but with enough strength in it to reach Manners. Lady Darriby-Jones felt a fraud at that moment; she often went on the rumblings of her gut, yet was holding Manners to account for doing exactly the same thing.

In the Battle of the Gut, Lady Darriby-Jones would win hands down, rounding up her opponents and delivering them into prisoner of war status.

"But you seemed determined to prevent me following up on the single lead we have," he said by way of justification as he signalled for the policeman not to step forward with handcuffs in hand.

"You mean the Sally angle?"

"Precisely."

"Red herring, dear Manners, a simple red herring." Lady Darriby-Jones seemed in total control as she explained that it was impossible for Sally Skinner's story to have relevance.

"How so? I mean, a sighting is a sighting, isn't it?"

"Let me show you, Chief Inspector. But first, please consider dismissing the staff before we have a riot on our hands."

Manners replied that, as he had identified his suspect, he saw no harm in letting the others go, but they were too incensed to listen to him, chanting 'Not milady, not milady' over and over again.

It took Lady Darriby-Jones to come to the edge of the balcony, resting her hands on the wooden banisters running around the entire library. When enough people saw her there, the chanting died down to a trickle and she was able to address them in true hero/ general/ emperor style.

"Dear members of staff, your loyalty touches my heart and I thank you for it. There's an expression:

The Truth Will Out

And I have no doubt that it will appear before too long. I'm going with the detective chief inspector now. No, listen please. I will go with the chief inspector because I want to demonstrate one thing to him. After I've fully demonstrated this, I believe he will regard me as innocent of these crimes, or at least, no longer the main suspect."

"We won't let you be carted off in chains," Baritone's voice raised above hers. Was he enjoying this? Certainly, the glint in his eyes and the glisten on his skin suggested just that.

"Nobody's going to be put in chains." But the voice of one man, albeit a detective chief inspector, was nothing compared to the noise of the rabble rising again, now chanting 'no chains, no chains' to a steady rhythm, with Baritone waving his arms around like an over-enthusiastic orchestra conductor.

"Quick, this way," Lord Darriby-Jones said, suddenly at her side in her hour of need and seeing no option but to reveal a secret he knew about the library. "There's another way out." He led them to a particular part of the upper story, pressed a button located behind a book on the history of the Darriby family, and a narrow doorway swung on a pivot to reveal a dark passage beyond. Once they had entered, he pressed another button and the door closed again. Several police officers reached for their lighters, so the scene became scattered dots of moving light.

"Late converts to the Church of England," Lord Darriby-Jones explained as he led the entire police party and his wife down the dark tunnel, which soon branched out into other tunnels.

"It's a priest's hole," Lady Darriby-Jones cried.

"More than that, an entire network of passages and hiding places. I believe it was created by an eccentric Darriby about twelve 'greats' ago. The story goes he used it once to hide a priest, then converted and from thereafter it became a way to disappear from his staff and family; it was a game to him."

"Why didn't you tell me about this?" she asked.

"Truth is, I forgot all about these passages. It must be thirty-five years since I last came down here. Mind the cobwebs."

It quickly became apparent that Lord Darriby-Jones didn't recall the myriad of passages as they wondered done some and back up others, at one point, almost stepping back into the library.

Lady Darriby-Jones began to imagine they were about to wander the passages until the last one of them dropped dead. If she had known about this secret network, she could have positioned chocolate and bottles of gin in different places, allowing sustenance to all who travelled therein.

But she hadn't known, not until now; one secret of Darriby Hall that had never been passed on. She contemplated, as she put one brown solid shoe in front of the other, why that had been the case, concluding that it was the slugs at fault.

"Dearest," she said at a pause where the main tunnel ended at a junction with two more, "why did you not tell me of these secret passages?"

"I forgot all about them, my dear, until I saw you in difficulty. The household staff were never going to let you be taken away by the police and suddenly a memory from my boyhood came back to me, offering a solution."

"I blame the slugs, dear. They've taken over your life completely."

"That's as may be," he replied, a particularly 'say nothing of meaning' string of words. "Now where do you want to go?"

"Into the American Quarters or as near as you can," she replied. The batch of half-a-dozen bedrooms and an antiquated bathroom that led off the main staircase gallery had had no particular name until christened a couple of days ago by the arrival of the American party. Half-a-millennium without a name and suddenly everyone knew them as the 'American Quarters'.

"Oh, why didn't you say so? That's easy." But it wasn't so easy to reverse a column of police officers in a narrow tunnel. Lady Darriby-Jones became a traffic marshal, ordering them to back up into a small alcove she remembered passing a moment earlier. There was a loud yowl as a lighter came too close to Manners, together with a slight smell of burnt flesh.

"Take that man's name, sergeant."

"Yes, sir." But how do you take your own name?

They made it eventually, coming out of the fireplace in the very room Lady Darriby-Jones needed them to be, the one that had, until recently at least, been occupied by one Harrison B. Potters, now lying on a slab somewhere waiting for a burial some five thousand miles from his place of birth.

Such is the complex migratory path of the human species.

They entered the room, the policemen busily brushing off dust and cobwebs from their uniforms, Lady and Lord Darriby-Jones too relieved to be out in the open to care for a little dirt.

"Hello," Lady Alice greeted them. "So Alfie was right then. You were coming here." Alfie realised just after these words that Lady Alice had, for the second time, referred to him by his first name. Things were looking up.

"How did you know?" Lady Darriby-Jones asked.

"Oh, that was simple. There's only three entrances and exits to the tunnels. The library, this room, and a scullery near the kitchens. It was really a process of deduction."

"You've known about these tunnels all the time?"

"Of course, know them like the back of my hand. I've even stashed gin and chocolate at strategic points, just in case."

"If only I'd known." Lady Darriby-Jones was thinking more about the gin and the chocolate than the escape route these passages offered.

But then, she always had her priorities in the right place.

Chapter Ten

"This is what I want to try," Lady Darriby-Jones explained when everyone had dusted themselves off sufficiently.

"You're not out of the woods yet, Lady Darriby," Manners replied, feeling an evident need to establish his authority. "I've still got you right in me sights."

"My sights," Lady Alice said flatly.

"Your sights too?" Manners sounded puzzled.

"No, the correct way to say it is 'my sights', not 'me sights'. I can't abide sloppy talk. Sloppy talk means…"

"Sloppy minds," Sergeant Fisher finished the saying for Lady Alice, earning a scowl from DCI Manners.

"As I was saying, I want to do a re-enactment of possible events to show the irrelevance of young Sally's statement."

"You've got ten minutes," Manners replied, as if the truth could be packaged and dribbled out in ten-minute slots.

"I'll need a little more than that. I think maybe sixteen minutes. What do you think, Alfie?"

"I've no idea, Lady Darriby-Jones. If I knew something of the context, I might be able to offer my opinion."

"Yes, quite so. I forgot to explain. Now, Mr Manners, how long did Sally say the gap was between the shot and the sighting of the figure running between the rhododendrons?"

"Sergeant Fisher, how long between the..."

"Three minutes at most, sir."

"That's important, Mr Manners, as I shall now demonstrate. Imagine for a moment that the killer is young and fit and knows his way around Darriby Hall." She turned to Alfie at that point and told him he was instrumental in this effort because he fitted the bill, being young, fit and aware of the layout of the house. "Let's assume you've just stabbed young Potters and you need to get away."

"I didn't and wouldn't..."

"We're assuming, Alfie, and you're playing a role. Bear with me. No one is going to arrest you because of a role you're playing now."

"Don't predict a no arrest scenario, 'coz I might just arrest every single one of you, the way this is going."

"Enough, enough, enough," Lady Darriby-Jones cried out, "Alfie, what route would you take to get out towards the rhododendrons out there?" She pointed out towards the bank of pale green bushes in the distance beyond the lawns.

"Well, let me see." Alfie went to the window. "The best way would be out here, onto the balcony and drop down to the ground."

"Alright, Alfie, can you do that for me?"

"Certainly, Lady Darriby-Jones." He turned back to the window and tried to open it. "Um, a problem. The window's stuck and I just can't get it open."

"You'll note, Mr Manners, that it's painted shut; that window hasn't been opened in an age."

"So, he would go to the next bedroom and drop down from there."

"Ah, two problems there. First, would our murderer really risk disturbing someone else straight after the dirty deed."

"He might do. Can't tell." Manners, as ever when faced with logic, went into a sulk.

"The other reason is more overpowering. Follow me." She marched towards the door and out into the narrow passageway, deciding to give a history lesson as she went. "This part of the house was the original, built in the mid-thirteenth century on the site of an old Saxon manor, so they believe. When the Darriby clan made pots of money during the reign of Henry VIII from the dissolution of the monasteries, even though they remained Catholic for a while, and again during Elizabeth's reign from a mixture of piracy and the early colonies, they built the new house on top of the old house, literally burying the old one in new stone and mortar. Many people would have torn down the old and started again but that just doesn't seem to be the Darriby way. Ah, here we are now. This is the Hammerstein bedroom. Further along is the other one occupied by Miss Bollinger." She went straight to the window after flicking on the light switch.

"Here's the little problem that escape through these rooms poses," she said, using her arms to invite the police contingent to take a look.

"What a drop," Sergeant Fisher said, "not even a drainpipe to slide down."

"I don't understand," Manners said, "we went up, what, five steps?"

"Six, sir, I counted them," Fisher said.

'Right, six then, but that drop must be fifty feet."

"The ground outside drops down on the way to the west wing, Mr Manners. It becomes two stories here with all the kitchens and pantries on the lower floor. Now the west wing was added by Lord…"

"Spare me the history lesson, Lady Darriby. So, our murderer didn't go out this way and the bathroom window is too small for anyone bigger than a midget. They must have gone into the main part of the house and then doubled back towards the rhododendrons."

"Synchronise your watches, gentlemen," Lady Darriby-Jones said, "I make it sixteen minutes to six in twenty seconds."

"Why are we doing this?"

"Because we're going to time Alfie on his desperate run from the murder scene to the rhododendrons. Three minutes is the target. Any gamblers amongst you?" The consensus was twelve minutes and Lady Alice started taking bets until Lady Darriby-Jones suggested that the main purpose was not to enrich her daughter but to make a point about the rhododendron run.

"Alright, I'm ready," said Alfie, taking off his jacket, loosening his tie and stretching like it was the four-forty-yard sprint he was limbering up for.

"What's your route going to be?" Sergeant Fisher asked.

"Well, I don't know, actually. I hadn't thought of that yet."

"It's obvious, Alfie," Lady Alice said. "Go into the main part of the house through the little door, along the main staircase gallery, down the main stairs, out the front door and west to the rhododendrons."

"No, that would take forever," Lord Darriby-Jones said, "better to head to the blue room. I know that window opens. There's a big drainpipe right outside that window. That will cut the time by..."

"No," said Alfie, "I mean, Lady Darriby-Jones, I shall go to the main landing and then head for the fire escape at the back of the house, rattle down there and then across the narrow stretch of lawn to where the..."

"Nonsense," and so it went on until Alfie stamped his feet and told the assembled party that he was the main actor in this particular scene and he would decide which route he would be going to take.

"So, which one will it be, then?"

"Through the front door and..."

"I knew it," claimed Lady Darriby-Jones. "You've selected the way Lady Alice wants you to go. I knew you would."

"Whatever," said a grumpy Manners, "it's time to make this dash or I'm going to arrest the lot of yer for wasting police time."

It was, indeed, time to start the mad dash; route decided, watches synchronised, runner warmed up, now to reveal the moment of truth.

"Ready, steady go."

Alfie was off, making good progress. The police, Lady Darriby-Jones and Lady Alice, crowded around the window in the room that Potters had briefly occupied.

"Gentlemen," Lady Alice said, "can we not come to an arrangement?"

Lady Darriby-Jones saw the look of interest on DCI Manners' face; he obviously thought Lady Alice was trying to bribe him in some way, and was very much enjoying the prospect of introducing another serious crime to Darriby Hall.

That is, until her next words.

"We're shorter than you great hulking bobbies. Can't we stand at the front by the window so you can see over our heads?"

The wall of blue parted like the Dead Sea and the two ladies took pole position by the window, standing square on so that Lord Darriby-Jones could see between their heads.

"Eight minutes and counting," Lady Alice said. She stood to gain fifteen shillings if it went over the twelve-minute mark.

"There he is," Lady Darriby-Jones called a moment later. He's through the front door and is coming down the steps. What time now?"

"Six minutes and forty-eight seconds."

"He's gonna do it." Manners forgot his own importance for a moment, getting sucked into the fun of it.

"No one can run across the drive and then the lawn in five minutes."

"He's fast, is that Alfie."

"One second over and I keep all the stakes," Lady Alice said, clearly exhibiting her competitive nature.

"Come on, Alfie, run like the wind."

"Ten seconds, nine, eight..." He wasn't going to make it.

"Five, four, three..."

It looked possible, but not when the gradient was taken into account. A bank led up to the rhododendrons and Alfie faltered at the last moment.

"Twelve minutes and eleven seconds."

"So, you see, Mr Manners, it isn't possible that the runner had anything to do with the murder. One body can't be in two places at the same time."

Chapter Eleven

"There's something I really don't understand," Manners said from the bed he had taken to sitting on, one of the two single ones pushed along separate walls that marked out the Hammerstein's bedroom. It was this separation of the beds that had led Lady Darriby-Jones to suspect that the Hammerstein's marriage might be a sham, although Manners, a bachelor of long standing, had dismissed this suggestion with considerable disdain, claiming many happily married couples chose to sleep in separate rooms. Lady Darriby-Jones knew this to be a fact but, despite her husband's snoring, couldn't imagine not snuggling up to him at night.

"What's that, DCI Manners?" Be magnanimous in victory, the little voice inside her said; after all, you may need the favour returned at some later date. But, it was an undoubted victory on the basis that Manners had been determined to arrest her before, something about her questionable dismissal of the sighting of the figure by the rhododendrons. Now, that she had convincingly evidenced no connection between the fleeting figure and the murder of Potters, the rudest policeman she had ever come across seemed disinclined to slip the handcuffs on her now.

"How it is that you were seen wondering around the house a little before three o'clock of the morning in question. There's no point in denying it, Lady Darriby, you were seen by Torino. We questioned the man and eventually he cracked." Lady Darriby-Jones imagined Torino under questioning for a moment, not believing he would 'crack' at anything that Manners could throw his way. They had bumped into each other in their dressing gowns and slippers, Torino embarrassed at (a) being seen improperly dressed, although Lady Darriby-Jones assured him that dressing gown and slippers were perfectly appropriate for three in the morning, and (b) the purpose behind his nocturnal wandering, to which Lady Darriby-Jones could only say 'snap'.

"Oh that, it's because of Mrs Britain. It's all her fault."

"Why's that and who's Mrs Britain?" Also, although Manners dared not ask this at the time, why was everything to do with the Darriby family so darned complicated?

"The substitute cook, of course, just while Mrs Stone is away visiting her sick mother. You see, Mrs Britain has to be the worst cook in Christendom, regularly giving her victim runny tummies or worse. Both Torino and I were seeking a finger or two of brandy to settle our tums. I persuaded Torino, eventually, to sit with me and I asked him about his childhood in Italy. Do you know he could see the Leaning Tower of Pisa from his bedroom window?"

"Lady Darriby, don't get me side-tracked on some incidental rubbish about Italian childhoods. Us policemen just need the facts, and that's a fact."

She didn't get his little joke, and neither did Manners because his play on words had been an accident, but Fisher gave out a great bellow of laughter until glared into silence by Manners. He was going to have to do something about Fisher's impudence. Perhaps set an example for the others?

"Still, you can see my dilemma, can't you, Lady Darriby?" This was dangerous ground and a part of him knew it; never expose your underside to the enemy. Was Lady Darriby the enemy? Yes, in terms of how he had felt at Sandham Court during the war. He had, foolishly it seems, imagined he would be welcomed as a captain in the Military Police, a commissioned officer, no less, and one with considerable police experience and several near encounters with danger to recount over port and cigars. Instead, he had felt the rough tongue of disdain on everything he had ever done.

And this all showed, plain as day, on his face every time Lady Darriby-Jones saw him.

For three long years while the war ground to a stalemate, making him ache to be back amongst the 'little people' and back in civvies as a detective inspector, angling his way for promotion, finally achieving the exalted heights of Detective Chief Inspector just last year.

Then to be sent to Darriby of all places, the mirror image of Sandham in many ways, and far from the sophistication and excitement of a detective in the city of Oxford.

"Yes, Mr Manners, I can see your dilemma only too clearly," said with more condescension than would fit in the pages of a Jane Austen novel. And felt by Manners too, such that his little boy lost expression made Lady Darriby-Jones vow to be more tolerant in the future.

"Still, must get on," he slapped his own thigh, not being able to reach his back, back-patting being something he particularly craved.

"What's next?" Lady Darriby-Jones asked, to which Manners shrugged as if she had deliberately let him down by proving her innocence; if only she had been a little less on the ball, he would have collected up his murderer by now and wrapped her in paperwork while shovelling her into the bars of the single cell at Darriby Police Station.

If only.

"What are you going to do about the latest find?"

"The latest find?"

"The gun in Mrs Hammerstein's handbag, of course." Not said with anything but genuine interest by Lady Darriby-Jones, yet the words became distorted across the ten feet they travelled, coming out as the schoolmistress asking one of her charges whether he had been paying proper attention.

Which he evidently had not been doing; vaguely he recalled something about a gun being found just as he had entered the library, fixated on carting off the prize of Lady Darriby-Jones to the dungeons of the Darriby police cells.

"The gun, yes, the gun. Run through the briefing again. There's a good girl, I mean lady." He could do the condescension line every bit as patronizing as that he perceived to have received. That thought puffed him up a bit after the bitter disappointment of his catch slipping off the line at the last moment.

Lady Darriby-Jones briefed him, knowing full-well that he hadn't bothered with understanding what was going on in the library on entering some hours ago, too bound up in his rush to make an arrest, any arrest to be able to say he had closed the case. Knowing also that Manners was the type to rush in again and again, grasping at straws where none existed.

Could you grasp at imaginary straws, or was that the very point of the saying? She didn't know, so put the question to one side, telling herself to concentrate on solving the case that lay before her.

More to prove her theory about Manners' deficiencies to herself than to seek justice, she concluded her thorough and detailed briefing of the discovery of the gun by asking him what he would do with this information.

"Why, make an immediate arrest," he said, as if anything else was frankly ridiculous.

"But who?"

"Mrs Hammerstein, of course," said as if it were as obvious as day was bright and night was dark, at least to those who had a brain on their shoulders.

"Have you considered that Mrs Hammerstein might have had the gun planted on her?"

"Tishwash," he replied, making up the word and loading it with disdain, also an element of pride at the quizzical look it put on Lady Darriby-Jones's face. "Let her explain how she was found with a Colt M1911 in her possession, the same gun from which the American bullet was fired.

"Well, you can't be sure it was the same gun, Mr Manners."

"Tishwash," he said again, rather liking the dismissive element weaved into this single word.

It came to Lady Darriby-Jones at that moment:

The Mystery of the American Gun

No, that wasn't quite right. It was the bullet that had thrust itself directly through the heart of poor Potters, ending his life and splitting the slumbering silence of Darriby Hall. What did they call a bullet in the States? At least what they called them in the detective novels she had read from time to time, second guessing on motive, means and method? With a delicious sense of irony, she amended her mystery title as follows:

The Mystery of the American Slug

She rather appreciated the play on words but decided not to try and explain her tittering to Manners who was too busy (a) congratulating himself on solving the murder in record time, (b) issuing orders at top volume from his on-the-bed control station and (c) evidently composing his report to his superiors and wondering how he might include the Chief Constable in his distribution list, this latter point evidenced by the way his smile grew as the words poured through his mind.

Chapter Twelve

A knock on the door of the Hammerstein bedroom disturbed all this intense planning issuing out from the detective chief inspector.

"Enter." One short word said that Manners was back in control of events, where he should be in his opinion.

In came Lord Baritone, as sheepish as any Lord Baritone ever got. A long chain of proud men stretched back into history, but this latest one had a distinctly apologetic look about him.

"Eh, I wanted to clear up a misunderstanding that seems to have unfortunately arisen," he said, hat circling in his fingers, only there was no hat; Barry Baritone was sworn off hats. The story he had once told Lady Darriby-Jones, when well into his fifth whisky, was of a sniper having taken his father's life. The Hon. Brigadier Baritone, also a Barry so affectionately known as 'Brig BarBar' by his friends, had been that rare example of a popular leader of men, but sadly cut down in the prime of life, another casualty from that dreadful war. His men had not rested in seeking revenge. When the sniper was captured by indignant soldiers of his brigade, who, to a man, had loved the deceased brigadier, they asked the sniper how he'd known who to pick on. The sniper had replied in pidgin English that they had standing instructions to go for the most elaborate hat every time.

Now, the current Lord Baritone stood in line to inherit two earldoms and several streets in London from his uncle who was childless following the same war, all three boys having gone either to sharpshooters hiding in no-man's-land, following their instructions to 'go for the officers', or to shell blasts and those wretched machine guns.

He now stood in line because others had fallen in line. The war had a lot to answer for and was best forgotten, put back in the box called history.

Baritone had been in his cups when he related this to Lady Darriby-Jones, but he clearly said he would willingly give up his vast inheritance if the war had not happened.

"Father wanted me to be a clergyman," he had slurred, "so that is what I would have become had the war not got in the way."

"DCI Manners," Baritone said, clearly feeling he had something to get off his chest.

"Not now, Lord Baritone. I've got more important things to worry about."

"But…"

"But me no buts, Baritone," Manners' rudeness fell upon the room like the sharpest scythe through grass. Or a guillotine in action. Lady Darriby-Jones couldn't understand it and vowed to have a comforting word with Baritone as soon as she could, Manners or no Manners.

"But..."

"Don't try me, man. I've got an arrest to make and got to be pretty snappish about it." He called for Sergeant Fisher, who Lady Darriby-Jones could see propping up the wall in the passageway outside the open door. He sighed on hearing the call, finished the cup of coffee he had got from somewhere, and placed cup and saucer on a small side table. Only then did he straighten up and put the load of his whole body back onto his feet, before calling out a, "coming sir, won't be a tick, sir."

It made Lady Darriby-Jones think about the word, 'sir'. It often signified respect, sometimes deeply held. Other times, it was a mere form of words, a pattern trotted out by those destined to serve others. Very occasionally, however, it was used by a 'master of attitude' to display the utter contempt held for a superior, leaving that superior totally unable to reprimand, yet knowing full well that they've been firmly put in their place.

Sergeant 'Haddock' Fisher was just such a master and he played his part perfectly.

"Sergeant, there you are. Get the men assembled. We're making an immediate arrest."

"Can I ask who, sir?"

"Mrs Hammerstein, of course."

"Because of the gun, sir?" That brought something home to Manners. He had not taken anything in about the gun the first time around, congratulating himself for being rather clever in getting Lady Darriby-Jones to run through the facts again for his benefit.

He had not heard about the gun, yet his sergeant had. How could that be? He would have to have words later with him about passing information up the chain of command. Right now, he had an arrest to make and that, as ever, gave him the warmest type of joy.

"Sir, I would urge caution. We suspect this Colt M1911 was the one used to kill Mr Potters, but we don't know for sure. Mrs Hammerstein has no obvious motive for killing a PhD student, and I suspect we would have a problem gathering sufficient evidence to make the charges stand, as at the present."

"What would you propose, sergeant?"

"That we hold off on the arrest until we've sent the handgun to ballistics. If they report a match, we reconsider our options. In the meantime, we withdraw, other than I stay around for 'routine enquiries' as it were. That way, the murderer relaxes and my 'routine enquiries' are actually considerably more; I can dig around with her ladyship's approval and see what I can unearth. Sometimes, a 'quietly, quietly approach' is better than thundering around, sir."

"My approval is granted, Sergeant Fisher," Lady Darriby-Jones said at once. She wanted to add that her assistance would be forthcoming as well, but thought better of that, knowing what reaction that would have from Manners.

"How will you keep them contained, sergeant? Have you thought of that?" Every time Manners asked a question, Lady Darriby-Jones thought there was an element of something else in his words. What was it now? Spite? Malevolence? Antagonism? A little of all those, perhaps?

"Yes, sir, all duly considered from every angle, sir." That was a touch of the old Fisher back. "I thought I'd issue a strict rule to stay within the grounds and our bods will have orders to arrest anyone straying off the premises."

There was a long pause while these arguments ran through Manners' mind.

"Very well, sergeant, carry on." His disappointment stood out a mile; he would have to wait to compose that report to his superiors. But the sergeant, however dumb and impertinent he was, had a point and DCI Manners hadn't got to the exalted senior ranks of the Oxfordshire Police Force by charging right in there.

Or had he?

"I'm going off duty," Manners said a few minutes later to anybody who was listening; nobody seemed to be. All the police officers were clustered around 'Haddock' Fisher as he gave out his instructions, just like the old days. Lady Darriby-Jones listened for a moment, noticing the respect the constables had for their sergeant, wondering whether they could ever hold DCI Manners in similar regard. She almost felt sorry for him but managed to curtail that particular emotion before it got hold; the man was a rat of the first order. It's just that sometimes you could, just about, feel some form of communion with the bad guy, even with a rat of the first order.

Then she gathered up her husband and daughter and announced it was time to get back to normal.

"Whatever normal is," Lady Alice said as they exited the American Quarter to head back to the library.

Lady Alice's words stayed with her mother as they descended the main staircase and crossed the hall to the library. Could they really act normally with a vicious killer in their midst? What if she, her husband, or her daughter were next on the list?

Chapter Thirteen

The semblance of normality is what Lady Darriby-Jones sought, and she achieved it in sorts. After a second day of being rounded up and herded into the library, the family, guests and staff were addressed briefly by Sergeant 'Haddock' Fisher, every person acutely aware that this glum-looking police officer was quite different to the volatile, incendiary of a man called DCI 'Rude' Manners who, rumour had it, had gone home in a sulk. Fisher spoke quietly and efficiently without rattling handcuffs or having his uniformed officers fingering the heavy truncheons they carried.

"Just one thing to remember, and this goes for everyone," he said, looking around the fifty-odd people assembled in the room. "I don't want anyone leaving the grounds of Darriby Hall. Is that understood? This is absolutely essential. We very likely have a killer in our midst and it is essential that we remain where we are until we track the blighter down."

A general murmuring indicated it was understood, but Fisher decided to take it a step further.

"PCs Fortune and Goode will be releasing people one by one in a moment. Each one of you will be required to sign an agreement I've drawn up whereby you accept the ban on proceeding outside the grounds of Darriby Hall, unless, of course, you have a desire to be arrested and held in police cells pending further enquiries." Lady Darriby-Jones thought it odd that the police always said quaint but, at the same time, semi-frightening phrases such as, 'not to proceed' and 'pending further enquiries'. He wondered whether they spoke like that at home, issuing verbiage such as, "Darling, I'm just proceeding to the public house for a drink or three. Will you be accompanying my person?"

"No, dearest, please proceed alone." This particular wife had been in the police force herself before meeting the constable she happily married, producing little constables at the rate of half-a-dozen in as many years.

Then PC Fortune walked shyly up to Lady Darriby-Jones; his father was assistant head gardener at Darriby Hall, a position he had held for twenty-seven years and didn't look likely to proceed off anywhere else in short order.

"Will you please sign the instructions, milady?"

"Happy to do so, Fortune. How's your sister, by the way? Has she recovered from that nasty accident?" Annie Fortune had been proceeding back from the pub one night earlier that summer with her boyfriend, Sydney Luck, when she had strayed into the sluggery of all places. The silly couple had decided that the glass-topped cages housing slugs by category and placed in a row, had been stepping stones and had ran along them. Young Syd had been wearing his boots and came out the other end with just a scratch or two, but Annie Fortune had worn her new stilettoes and had to have fourteen shards of glass taken out of her feet by an irritated village doctor from the cottage hospital set up with an endowment given by Darriby's great grandfather.

Back in those long-lost days when money grew on trees. Even with the Jones fortune, Lady Darriby-Jones knew those affluent times were long gone. She sometimes felt their role was to manage a gentle decline while a few, like Baritone for instance, became richer and richer.

Like Baritone, now there was a man she needed to see, to ask about the matter he had come to confess to Manners about. Manners had cut him off short, brushing all concerns aside, but Lady Darriby-Jones knew there was something in it.

"Fortune, have you seen Lord Baritone anywhere?"

"No, milady. Let me check with PC Goode and see whether he's on his list." He returned a minute later and confirmed that Lord Baritone has muscled his way to the front of those being released by PC Goode and been the first to check out, scribbling his signature as little more than a large 'B' with a squiggle to follow.

"Does Goode know where he went?"

"No, milady. Just that he was in a terrific hurry."

It was at that precise moment that Sally issued a cry. She had been standing in the window, patiently waiting for her turn to be released.

"There it is again," she cried, turning forty heads as one.

"What again?" Lady Darriby-Jones asked as she strode across the library to gain the same vantage point as Sally.

"The same person as what I saw on the morning of the murder," Sally replied, forgetting and then hastily adding a 'milady' to her sentence.

Lady Darriby-Jones had one irritation she couldn't get over, that being for the last seven years, she had needed reading glasses. At first, she had fought it, selecting only books with larger print and then discretely keeping a magnifying glass in her skirt pocket. Eventually, Lady Alice had caught her squinting at a menu in a restaurant in Oxford, opting for the safety of saying she would have the same as her daughter.

"It's because you can't read the menu, isn't it, mother?"

"They've made it deliberately small, just like the portions," she had complained. This cut no ice with Lady Alice, who found time that very afternoon to drag her mother to an optician run by a tiny man with the thickest glasses ever.

Two weeks later, Lady Alice, not trusting her mother, took her back to collect her very first pair of spectacles.

When she told this tale at the dinner table, inevitably one of the guests would ask how her long-range vision shaped up.

"It's absolutely perfect, better than perfect, in fact," Lady Darriby-Jones would call down the dining table.

That's because it was, and she used that better than perfect vision right then, to centre in on the running figure that had almost reached the rhododendrons.

The Mystery of the American Slug

"I do believe it's Baritone," she muttered. "Yes, I'd know that strange lope anywhere."

"But what…?" The question came from Fisher and the implication was obvious.

"He's either meeting someone or leaving for the village."

"I'm going down there now," Fisher said. "Goode, come with me."

"No, sergeant, let me go," Lady Darriby-Jones said. "I'll get to the bottom of this if it's the last thing I do."

"What if he's violent?" Fisher asked, clearly thinking of a connection between Baritone and murder.

"I'll take Alfie with me," she replied.

"And me," Lord Darriby-Jones spoke up, "I'm not going to let you go into danger when I could be by your side." At that moment, she realised just how much she had come to love her husband, for all his sluggish ways. Her heart danced so far out of her body, she swears it met his dancing too.

"Count me in too," Lady Alice said.

"How do we approach this situation?" Lady Darriby-Jones asked her two male protectors plus female, as they started to cross the vast lawn. She knew she would make the final decision, but wanted contributions first.

"Charge him down and confront him," Darriby said.

"Yep, that's the only way," Lady Alice agreed.

"Edge around the lawn and keep out of sight while approaching him. Then we can see what he's up to." That was Alfie's suggestion.

It was also the one they adopted, much to the disgust of father and daughter.

As they approached the rhododendrons, Lady Darriby-Jones directed them to take cover while she crept forward, skirting around the big, green leaves, wondering what the next step might reveal. She wanted to scout alone, but every time she turned to look around, the backup team had crept along behind her.

"Sshh," she had to say quite a few times. Lord Darriby-Jones, in particular, seemed incapable of stepping quietly, making her wonder whether the slugs he so diligently cared for used to complain bitterly about 'old thunder boots' coming along again. She just spotted Baritone in the distance, weaving in and out of the bushes, therefore hard to keep tabs on. Then, Lord Darriby-Jones trod on a dry stick and the crack of breaking wood seemed louder than a pistol shot.

"What's that?" came Baritone's voice from behind a particularly large bush; Lady Darriby-Jones knew that there was a quaint bench just there, out of sight now, but when you went past the bush, it sort of invited you in.

Many a time, Lord and Lady Darriby-Jones had enjoyed a cuddle there while their servants searched high and low for the aristocratic fugitives. In later days, those same servants had learnt not to search too hard; everyone deserved a bit of privacy from time to time.

"Must be a squirrel," said a female voice and not an aristocratic one at that. Lady Darriby-Jones looked back at her team and saw the hackles rising down Lady Alice's back. She moved forwards. Lady Darriby-Jones managed to restrain her.

"Hush, Ali, you never liked him anyway."

"That's not the point," she hissed back.

"Now there's a hissing noise," Baritone said. "Will I need to save my princess from the snakes that abound around here?"

It was too late now. Lady Alice could pour disdain by the bucketful, but could she take it? Any slight made her turn red, trembling in anger like a berserk in the books about Vikings fighting Saxons and all that.

Before Lady Darriby-Jones could act to restrain her, she was out from behind her bush and making rapid tracks for the source of her anger.

Surprisingly, Lord Darriby-Jones was right behind her, holding a stick he'd pulled right out of the ground from a coppice of hazel.

It was the countdown to war.

Chapter Fourteen

What made it worse, the girl was exceedingly pretty with long legs and the most beautiful flowing jet-black hair with natural shades of deep chestnut that glistened in the September sun. She had a straight nose that turned up just a bit towards the end, like a ski ramp Lady Darriby-Jones had seen once in the Alps. Her husband had briefly taken to skiing, before he found out that he had not one jot of co-ordination between any part of his body or mind; several bones threatened to break until Lord Darriby-Jones saw sense and settled on the science of slugs instead.

Lady Darriby-Jones's ire was raised when she saw the man of her life staring at this Aphrodite-like vision, although she was fairly sure that Aphrodite was usually depicted as a blond.

At least on the stage. She was about to say something to him, anything, then she realised in a flash that his fascination for the dark-haired figure before him had nothing to do with lust and everything to do with anger for his daughter; she told herself off silently for not being in communion with the man she had shared the last twenty years with.

"I see introductions are called for," Baritone said, somewhat embarrassed but he wasn't about to let that worry him too much. "This is Stella..."

"Not Stella Johnson," Lady Darriby-Jones interrupted, it suddenly clicking. Lots of things seemed to be clicking at that moment.

"The one and same, Lady Darriby-Jones," she said with a sweet smile that caused Lady Alice to blow another gasket.

"What are you doing?" Lord Darriby-Jones finally found his voice.

Everyone looked at him and then to Lord Baritone, following Lord Darriby-Jones's icy stare. "You're supposed to be courting my daughter, Good Lord, man."

"It's nothing, really."

"Nothing? Playing second fiddle behind my back, in my own backyard." When Lord Darriby-Jones lost it, his metaphors went flying out of the window.

"Just a bit of fun, really."

"Really?" It was a toss-up as to who was the most enraged, father or daughter, with trembling limbs and shades of blotchy red competing to win top prize.

Then Stella joined in.

"You said I was everything, Bar Bar. You said I was the most important thing in your life. Now, the moment it turns sour, I'm suddenly nothing?"

Baritone may be arrogant, abrasive and argumentative, but give him his credit; he knew when he was beaten.

He looked a moment longer at them all, alternating between all those he had let down, then he turned on his heels and sprinted towards the village.

"Hey, wait, stop!" shouted Lady Darriby-Jones as Baritone moved his body like a big cat, slinking and sleek.

"Can't stop," he cried, his voice becoming a squeak of nerves and bluster, "got to run," he called over his shoulder.

"Wait a moment," came from behind them, then, "stop that man."

Lady Darriby-Jones knew that voice and didn't need to turn to see 'Haddock' Fisher making great strides across the lawn, reaching the rhododendrons as Baritone left them out on the village side.

He would have got away to freedom, except for Alfie Burrows, who afterwards couldn't say what or why he had done it, but he did. Moving like lightning, he flew after the fleeing lord and threw himself at him in what Lady Darriby-Jones later said was a perfect rugger tackle.

Baritone was half as big again as Alfie in terms of overall mass, made up of four inches in height, three in breadth and the rest in pure muscle.

But the bigger they are....

"Where did you learn that, young man?" said Lady Darriby-Jones as Baritone was cuffed and led away, ironically in the same direction he was trying to escape down, but this time his destination was a date with the inside of a police cell, the only police cell for several miles around.

"I... don't know, Lady Darriby-Jones. It just sort of came to me."

"We'll have to have you in the team, you know?"

"The team?"

"Darriby Hall against the village every November." She turned to a panting Sergeant Fisher and asked whether it had not been a pretty good show.

"Yes," he gasped, "an excellent performance, Mr Burrows."

"What are you going to do with Lord Baritone?" Lady Darriby-Jones asked.

"Well, he's been arrested and we'll get a statement from him. Let him cool off a bit in the cells, probably release him tomorrow."

"May I walk down to the police station with you and him, sergeant? I know it's against the rules to leave the grounds but with your permission...?" The truth was, Lady Darriby-Jones (a) wanted to get away from her family for a short while, and (b) desired to be somewhere else to Darriby Hall, even if only for the twenty minutes it would take to walk to the station.

"Yes, I don't see why not. I'll need a statement from you, anyway."

"Not from the others?"

"I don't see any need to bother them, milady, do you?" Fisher clearly didn't want the emotional baggage of two more Darriby-Joneses. This theory of Lady Darriby-Jones's was evidenced a moment later when the police party plus Lady Darriby-Jones and Lord Baritone started their march for the police station. Lord Darriby-Jones, who she knew to be much affronted by Baritone's behaviour at weaselling his way back into Darriby Hall on the grounds of being totally smitten by Lady Alice, then having a dalliance with Stella Johnson from the village on the side, strode up to Baritone, a menacing look on his face.

"Baritone, I want you off my property, never to return." Baritone looked surprised, about to reply to his host, but Lord Darriby-Jones had turned and, in good police imitation, was proceeding at pace away from the scene.

That's when Lady Darriby-Jones realised that Lady Alice and Stella had also disappeared. She wandered around the rhododendron patch and then stopped when she heard, but did not see, them.

"Take that," came Alice's voice, "and that and that and that." Whether 'that' was a blow to the body or a kick on the shins, she never found out. Indeed, knowing her daughter, it was likely to be a combination of both.

Poor Stella Johnson, Lady Darriby-Jones thought, there's really a lot to be said for looking rather plain. She was paying for her stunning looks in spades. And how would she ever explain the ripe set of bruises to her father that evening?

The journey to the police station was uneventful. Lady Darriby-Jones resisted a little dance-led ceremony when she stepped out of the grounds and into the village, sobered by the realisation that even the village was largely Darriby property, so it was not as if she were going to places unknown. Baritone hung his head the whole walk, presumably confused; one moment he was having his cake and eating it, the next there was no cake on the table, just some hurt pride from having been brought down by Burrows in such splendid fashion. Fisher panted most of the way, only slowly regaining his breath; his pursuit had been rapid and forthright, only a pity it hadn't been spent in chasing down the murderer.

For one thing Lady Darriby-Jones had worked out during the journey from rhododendrons to police station lock up, is that Baritone was not the murderer, mainly because he couldn't be in two places at once. He clearly had been in the bushes, making his way to a rendezvous with Stella Johnson at the time when the fatal shot had been fired.

The Mystery of the American Slug Remained just that—
a Mystery.

They arrived at the police station and Sergeant Fisher immediately placed a confused, hence subdued, Lord Baritone in the single cell.

"I'll just call the boss," he said, "and tell him of developments. Goode, be so kind as to put the kettle on. I'm sure Lady Darriby-Jones must be gasping."

She was, but would never admit to it. The others, she thought, might well gasp, but she had her position to think of and would never deign to be seen gasping in public.

Fisher came back a moment later, having used Manners' office to telephone the boss at home.

"Milady," he said hesitantly, "I rather think the detective chief inspector got the wrong end of the stick." Was that a twinkle of enjoyment she noted in the sergeant's eye?

"The wrong end of the stick—how so, sergeant?"

"He thinks we've got the murderer when we haven't. In fact, he kept banging on about it, milady, saying his methods had triumphed over..."

"Yes, triumphed over what?"

"Triumphed over you, milady, only he didn't refer to you as a lady, milady." There it was again, a distinct twinkle in the eyes and it came from a burst of pleasure and enjoyment at the hole his unsavoury boss was undoubtedly digging for himself.

Chapter Fifteen

Manners had his moment of glory, followed rapidly, as so often happens, by a thundering big fall. Lady Darriby-Jones considered it, on balance, to be his own fault, although Sergeant 'Haddock' Fisher had an element of culpability, more so because he obviously enjoyed his boss's subsequent embarrassment.

Not that he could have planned that, unless, by some strange circumstance, Haddock was, himself, the murderer.

While he was undoubtedly mischievous towards the boss imposed on him by the higher-ups, who ought to have known better than to upset the apple cart, Haddock Fisher just didn't have the personality to push that apple cart, driver and all, over the cliff into the disused Darriby Quarry, leaving it smashed upon the rocks lying below.

In other words, he might be insubordinate, but never to the point of aiming a gun at point-blank range. He was one man who would never be a murderer, Lady Darriby-Jones considered.

No, on balance, Manners brought it upon himself. He didn't need to call a press conference for that very evening, but he did, hosting it in the village hall, thereby forcing the Darriby Girl Guides to find a different location for their weekly meeting. He also didn't need to announce to the world that the murderer was locked up in Darriby police station, feeling very sorry for himself, but he did this too. Not only did he do it but he enjoyed every minute, Lady Darriby-Jones noted while standing at the back near the store room so she wouldn't be a focal point. His triumphant phrases rang through the hall, lots of mention of apprehending, pursuit, and then the concept of the methodical process of deduction being at the heart of good policing.

With all the credit to himself. She cringed from the shadows as Manners banged on about what good leadership in policing could do to crime in small rural locations, snorting at the hypocrisy of a man who knew nothing about procedure and methodology, preferring to jump to rapid conclusions every time.

She slipped away and went quietly and alone back through the shrubbery to Darriby Hall. There she found both members of her family still fuming, indulging themselves by constantly reminding each other of the audacity of Baritone. She left them to it and went in search of Alfie, who she found in the west wing, sitting thoughtfully by the empty fireplace in one of the lesser-used sitting rooms.

"Quite a day," she said, when he immediately rose on entering the room.

"Yes, quite a puzzle," he replied, only sitting when Lady Darriby-Jones was herself comfortably seated.

"Why so?" she asked, wondering if that was the right way to pose the question. Now that over twenty years separated her from any remote attempt to provide an education, she wished she had applied herself more in her broken school journey. What it would be to know about things other than Darriby, to have a wider knowledge of the world than northwest Oxfordshire and the Highlands of Scotland, where their other home was situated.

"Well, eh," Alfie looked embarrassed, unsure of how to say what was on his mind.

"Out with it," she said abruptly, then adding with a little more tenderness that a problem shared was a problem solved.

Or halved or something like that. Education again; it kept cropping up.

"If I may speak frankly, Lady Darriby-Jones," he said hesitantly.

"It's the only way, my lad, out with it as frank as you like."

"It's just that your daughter so evidently has feelings for Lord Baritone and I had hoped she might develop some in a different direction." Well, that wasn't exactly frank, but Lady Darriby-Jones caught the meaning after half-a-mo. of consideration. The question was, what to do about it? Then she knew; pride was causing trouble once more.

"I don't think that girl has feelings for Barry," she said with growing confidence as her thoughts developed into a whole packaged argument. "I think her pride was hurt by something rotten and that gets to a girl, you know. There's nothing worse to the average female than declaring your love on one level while playing the field on another, however casual that playing around might be."

"Well, you know her better than any, Lady Darriby-Jones," he replied, making Lady Darriby-Jones wonder whether anyone knew Lady Alice at all.

"Stay on course, Alfie. You never know. The worst thing you can do is give up on a situation. Now, let me tell you about the great big gaping hole DCI Manners has not only dug for himself but jumped right into."

The cry rang out through the dark, moonless night, two hours before dawn. Correction, not a cry but a heart-rendering shriek expressing pure agony, mixed with a large dose of shock. A mere cry wouldn't have penetrated from the American Quarter quite so far across the family bedrooms in the main part of the house, nor upstairs to where Torino laid his head for a few brief hours every night.

Lady Darriby-Jones knew Torino had been woken by the shriek because he bumped into on the narrow balcony that led to the small door that she had some difficulty getting through these days.

The door to the American Quarter.

"Did you hear?" that was Lady Alice, asking the same question that Alfie posed just a moment later. That meant only Lord Darriby-Jones had slept through it, the penetrating noise not sufficient to pierce his rumbling snores.

"It came from in there," Torino said. "Perhaps milady would like me to investigate first?"

"And miss all the action? No way, Torino." She opened the door and tried to step through.

"There we are, mother," Lady Alice gave her a push and she slid through as if coated in butter or oil.

Lady Darriby-Jones rushed to the first bedroom of the three in this section of the house, opened the door to find a terrible scene laid out on the bed before her, only revealing the full extent of the horror when she found the light switch and flicked it on.

The white sheets were red with spilt blood; the question was whose blood? Two figures lay face down on the bed. Neither Mr nor Mrs Hammerstein were moving.

"Call the police," she cried to whoever was following. Torino took a moment to take in the scene and left the room, bound for the telephone in the study.

Alfie was the one who was most impressed; going around the bed by giving it a wide berth, he stooped and felt the pulse of Mr Hammerstein, followed by his wife.

"They're both alive," he said.

"I'll get Torino to get an ambulance," Lady Alice said, clearly impressed with Alfie's initiative; Lady Darriby-Jones had time to witness a distinct 'that's the sort of man to have around in a crisis' look sent Alfie's way.

"We better try and see who's bleeding," Alfie said, "although I'm not sure if we should move the bodies in case we cause further damage."

"Or mess up the crime scene," Lady Darriby-Jones replied, thinking and staring hard. "Oh," she continued, "that's it. It must be Mr Hammerstein's blood."

"How can you tell?"

"Mrs Hammerstein, or whatever her real name happens to be, is holding the knife. That means the odds are that she's the one inflicting the damage."

"Yes, but what happened to her then to knock her out?"

"It's a mystery," Lady Darriby-Jones replied, because it really was:

The Mystery of the American Slug

To give the man credit, Manners was up there in ten minutes. He too stared at the scene, just like Lady Darriby-Jones. However, she surmised that his thought-pattern would be a little different to hers. This was demonstrated by the smiling, but breathless, figure of Sergeant Fisher arriving twenty steps behind his boss.

"Ah, it seems like we have a problem with solving our murder case, sir," he said. "Now, how will we explain this to the press and to the big bods in Oxford?"

"It's er... well, we'll.... I mean..."

There was no answer. Manners tried a few feeble excuses, running along the lines of, first, pure coincidence, then accomplices, but the credibility of each of his ideas was such that Manners quickly moved on to the next hopeless explanation.

The Mystery of the American Slug

"Perhaps, what's happened is..."

And then Mrs Hammerstein moved, thus saving the day for Manners, giving him someone to arrest.

"What?" she said as she sat on the bed and saw the party standing around them. "Why? Where's..." That's the point at which she noticed two things. First, the body of her husband. Second, the knife in her right hand.

Manners told Fisher to read out her rights and Fisher replied, in suitably insolent manner whether he wouldn't prefer to have the honour as he had solved the case, apparently.

"Just do it, sergeant. Goode, clear the room."

"The ambulance will be arriving, DCI Manners," said Alfie. "They're both alive."

"Do you think I can't see that? Clear the room, Goode. We'll let the stretcher crew in later. I need to have Mrs Hammerstein under arrest, pronto."

When Lady Darriby-Jones was bugged by something, it fairly bugged her to death, she being an all or nothing type of person. Thus, she hung around the doorway to the bedroom as Mrs Hammerstein was led off, presumably to share the single cell that the Darriby Dungeon boasted, for Lord Baritone was the criminal in current residence.

"Mr Manners, a word, please."

"Not now, Lady Darriby. Please, just back off and give the police some room to do their job."

Lady Darriby-Jones did back off, all the way to the little door that opened from the American Quarter to the balcony over the main staircase. She had to squeeze against the bannisters as the ambulance crew came rushing up the stairs, guided by an excited Torino.

"I think tea's called for," she said to Torino as they left him behind.

"Yes, milady."

"I'll take it in the breakfast room. I'm just waiting to have a word with the chief inspector."

"Very good, milady."

She did have her second chance with Manners, just after the stretcher team bore Mr Hammerstein away, an oxygen mask covering his face.

"Will he live?" she asked.

"Quite likely," the lead medic replied. "You see, it's a superficial wound. They're always the worst for blood."

"Ah, Mr Manners, I must have a word with you," she said a moment after the stretcher reached the hall below.

"Must you?"

"Yes, you see, I don't think Mrs Hammerstein is our culprit."

"Hang about," he almost shouted, "she was caught with a knife in her hand and you don't think she's guilty? Are you just trying to undermine me?"

"Not at all, Mr Manners, just trying to stop you getting into another fix," she replied a little huffily, before going down her stairs and to her breakfast room where her cup of tea waited for her.

Manners was making a fool of himself all over again. Was there a prize for the most bumbling policeman ever?

Chapter Sixteen

Lady Darriby-Jones' suspicions that all was not right with the assumption of guilt concerning the confused and concussed Mrs Hammerstein were endorsed by Haddock Fisher, who hung around when Manners left, charged with interviewing Miss Betty Bollinger. She had seen and heard nothing, having slept through the piercing scream, satisfactorily explained to Fisher and Lady Darriby-Jones by the earplugs she always wore at night, but had misplaced that morning when Lady Darriby-Jones asked to see what type they were.

"You see, Miss Bollinger, my husband snores for England and..."

"He does what?" she seemed incredulous that there was such a sport as snoring, let alone international fixtures.

"Oh, it's just a saying, Miss Bollinger. It means he snores along with the best of them."

"So, snoring's seen as a good thing here in England?"

"Now, it quite drives me mad at night. It's just another saying, Miss Bollinger. Shall we move on? I was only interested to see the type of ear plugs you use as mine are as ineffectual as a..." No, she wouldn't go on. It was too tiring to explain everything over again, especially before breakfast.

Just as this fruitless exercise was concluding, Torino entered the library to inform them that (a) breakfast was ready and (b) there was a 'telfono' call for Sergeant Fisher. Lady Darriby-Jones quite naturally headed out with the sergeant, destination the study; after all, it was her telephone.

"Yes sir, yes sir." Lady Darriby-Jones just stopped herself, adding, 'three bags full, sir', mainly because she realised that it was a pretty sober conversation.

"He's been summoned," Haddock said when he put down the receiver, which Torino immediately started polishing.

"To Oxford?" she asked.

"Yes, exactly. To see the higher-ups. You see, there's clearly a... how do I put it?"

"I think the right phrase is a credibility gap."

"Yes," said Haddock, smiling now at the thought, "you see he gave a press conference yesterday evening saying he had a certain man under arrest and now he had to explain why the man has meta-somethinged into a woman."

"Yes, meta..." but she couldn't put her finger on the right word either, "like caterpillars and butterflies."

The Mystery of the American Slug

"Exactly," he replied. "Lady Darriby-Jones, might I ask a terrific favour?"

"Ask and if it's in my power you shall have it," Lady Darriby-Jones replied, thinking those words came straight out of a play she'd seen once on an infrequent London trip. Their London house had been rented out some years ago. Not, thankfully, due to a need for the cash, but because neither Darriby-Joneses particularly liked the big smoke, although the theatre could be rather fun.

"The detective chief inspector told me to interview Mrs Hammerstein while he was unavoidably called to Oxford for urgent 'strategy talks'. I just wondered whether you'd be willing to accompany me to the station and sit through the interview with me."

"No can do, I'm..." But with a twinkle in her eye, it being fun to get one over the man who happily plagued his boss morning, noon and night.

"What? I thought you might find it interesting."

"It's not that, sergeant, it's just that I'm not allowed to leave the immediate vicinity of Darriby Hall and wouldn't want to be thrown in jail like poor..."

"You have permission, Lady Darriby-Jones. Truth is, we need your help in this case or it'll still be unsolved, even if they send their best brains down from Oxford." The implication was stark; Manners might be the rudest policeman in England, but he certainly wasn't the smartest.

"Happy to do so," she replied, absolutely delighted to be included, "but first things first, there's breakfast waiting."

"Oh, well, I'll just chop along to the police station," Fisher said.

"Not if you value your life sergeant, there's breakfast aplenty here."

"No, it's no trouble at all, Lady Darriby-Jones, I'll be on my…"

"Mrs Stone is back. She arrived yesterday."

"Then I'd love to stay. Shall I proceed to the servants' hall?"

"Yes, sergeant, proceed away, while I'll proceed Miss Bollinger and my family to the breakfast room."

Lady Darriby-Jones had another reason she wanted to be at the station. Knowing her daughter's wounded pride, she thought it advisable that Barry Baritone depart from Darriby and return to wherever Baritones resided when not staying, and irritating, their country hosts. No doubt he'd be back at some point, exactly like a bad penny, rolling up and gathering no moss, or whatever the saying was. People like that always turned up again, she thought, feeling something midway between fondness at his personality and disgust at his recent treatment of Alice.

After their respective breakfasts, Lady Darriby-Jones and Sergeant Fisher spent a pleasant thirty minutes walking to the police station, the time devoted to a summary of the case so far.

"I just don't think it's Mrs Hammerstein," Lady Darriby-Jones said on emerging from the rhododendrons. "I think it's too much human nature to get rid of the knife rather than grasping it tightly, as if you wanted to be blamed."

"So, following that logic, is it likely she's been framed?"

"Yes, exactly what I'm starting to think, sergeant. Someone, having killed Mr Potters with a slug from the gun we found, has gone on to try and stab to death Mr Hammerstein, while placing the blame, by way of the bloodied knife, on Mrs Hammerstein, or whatever her real name is, because I've known for a while that these two don't represent some blissful wedded union."

"Perhaps a union in crime, Lady Darriby-Jones." But she shook her head, still unconvinced. They were acting as a team for some reason, but not as criminals, just as they weren't a happily married couple.

Before they arrived at the police station, they could hear Baritone's loud voice from the other end of the short lane that led from the High Street to the police station; actually a mix of various excited voices, but with Baritone's to the fore.

They both heard the tale going on, something to do with shooting pheasants with a rickety old musket that couldn't be relied on to hit a barn door at twenty paces.

"And then my whole world blew up in my face. Oh, hello Lady Darriby-Jones, how nice to see you."

This illustrated what she liked about the man; he lived for the moment. She couldn't forgive or forget the enormous slight to her daughter, but that didn't mean she couldn't like the man.

"Not in your cell anymore?" she asked.

"No, rather upset about that. I was looking forward to a lie-in this morning and, what do you know, I get, instead, a rude awakening long before dawn, old army days and that rot. I was tossed out of my luxury accommodation to make way for another and then forced to camp out here in the break room."

"I'm so sorry for the inconvenience," Fisher said, "now might I trouble you to keep your voices down. In fact, it might be time to leave, Lord Baritone. Far from it for me to break up a party but I have some important police work to do. I've got to catch a real murderer, you know."

In contrast to the exuberance of Baritone, Eliza Hammerstein could only be described as quiet and serious. She confessed everything within minutes of the interview starting.

Only not quite the confession Manners would have expected.

Chapter Seventeen

"My name's not Eliza Hammerstein," she said, "and I'm not the wife of Mr Hammerstein. God," she suddenly exclaimed, "is he alright?"

"We don't know," Sergeant Fisher said, "but the ambulance crew thought it was just a superficial wound. Apparently, they're the worst for bleeding." Lady Darriby-Jones smiled at the sergeant's repetition of something he'd just learnt that morning, trotting it out as if he'd known it his whole life.

"So, the questions have to be why, how and what, as in what on earth's being going on?" Lady Darriby-Jones said, trying to focus the interview on something that might progress the case.

"You know that I'm English," the person who was not Mrs Hammerstein but had not yet provided an alternative, announced.

"That much we had just about grasped," the sergeant announced back, showing that he could do sarcasm when the situation called for it. "Perhaps you could be good enough to let us know your real name, just out of idle curiosity, of course, nothing to do with the fact that we're seeking a cold-blooded killer."

"That's not me," she replied, stiffening somewhat at Fisher's attitude. "But, I do see that I owe you an explanation, although that means breaking my client confidentiality."

"Client confidentiality? Next, you'll be telling us you're a private detective." This was said by Fisher with a tone that he'd heard it all before. Perhaps he had listened to plays on the wireless, but Lady Darriby-Jones hushed him, knowing that the average village copper spent his days keeping the peace between warring neighbours and locking up drunks to cool off overnight; it's unlikely that Haddock Fisher, likeable as he was, had experience much beyond the average.

"Actually, I am. We call ourselves investigators rather than detectives; it just seems a little more accurate description."

"Shall we start with your real name?" Lady Darriby-Jones suggested.

"It's Lucy Williamson of..."

"Williamsons and Sons," Fisher interrupted, before his mouth started in fish mode, opening and closing in wonder.

"That's correct, well almost. The correct title of the firm is Williamsons and Sons and Daughter. I've been working away in the firm for over twenty years and am a director alongside Daddy and my two bros."

"You've worked for the Darriby family before, haven't you?" Lady Darriby-Jones was firing on all cylinders now.

"Yes, years ago. That's why Lord Darriby-Jones recognised me, but couldn't place me. It was my first job. I was hired by the late Lord Darriby to investigate whether his other son, the one who would have inherited had he not died sadly at Mafeking, had any illegitimate children."

"He had at least one," Lady Darriby-Jones replied, thinking back to the previous mystery.

"Yes, PC Frank Hoosish, otherwise known as Frankly Useless. The late lord knew about him, but subsequent to that discovery, I was hired to determine whether there were any more."

"Did you find any?"

"Half a dozen possibilities, Lady Darriby-Jones, but nothing of any substance. Then the old lord died and your husband took over. It had been a personal commission, so it ended when the late Lord Darriby shuffled Heavenward. I've always supposed, being a religious person, that everything becomes known when one reaches Heaven, God being too kind to keep secrets from us."

"An interesting theory, Miss Williamson. Perhaps hell is the opposite. That's to say it's where all the things we've been dying to know when alive are still denied us in death. I can imagine the frustration to be every bit as painful as real torture. But we digress, interesting though it is. That explains the past, but what of the present?"

"Well, about that, I'm not satisfied that I've maintained the standards inherent in my profession. But the whole story goes back a way in time and distance, so may I suggest a cup of tea, sergeant? Some biscuits would be nice too. Remember, I've not had any breakfast yet."

"I can do better than that Miss Williamson," Haddock Fisher said, rising from his chair, "I live three doors down and Mrs Fisher does a powerful job with kippers, making a breakfast fit for a king, or rather a queen, I should say. I'll just pop along and ask her to 'rustle up some grub' as they say in the wild west."

"What better way to start the day than a kipper breakfast," Lucy replied. "Please pass on my thanks to dear Mrs Fisher."

With the sergeant gone about his duty to provide a hearty breakfast to those in his charge, however temporarily, especially the pretty ones, in which category the private investigator could definitely be included, Lady Darriby-Jones sought to clarify a personal point.

"Did you really find no substantial evidence of my late brother-in-law's dalliances and offspring resulting?"

"Well, here's the thing, Lady Darriby-Jones, when your husband inherited, subsequent to his brother's death followed by that of his father, he wrote to my father—me being a very junior investigator at that time—and asked that the files be destroyed and all investigations cease immediately. He included a handsome cheque in recompense for our services to date, but my father, being a man of honour..."

"Of course, but do go on."

The Mystery of the American Slug

"Being a man of honour, he burnt the papers relating to the case in our garden. So, the only way to determine whether there are any more half-Darribys running around in the world would be to start the whole investigation again and I'm not sure the present lord would approve of such an exercise. Ah, here's the sergeant back. What news of the promised breakfast, sergeant? You do know it's against the law to promise a girl breakfast and then go back on the deal, don't you? I think the penalty is to be hung drawn and quartered, or is that for treason?"

Both the sergeant and Lady Darriby-Jones chuckled at her joke. Sergeant Fisher assured her that he would not dare cross any lady over the matter of her kipper breakfast, while Lady Darriby-Jones contemplated an interesting fact.

Or rather, two facts intertwined. First, she had not been drawn at all to the personality of Mrs Hammerstein. Second, she liked Miss Williamson a lot.

"Alright," said Sergeant Fisher, as Lucy finished her breakfast and they all sipped at steaming tea in such big mugs that Lady Darriby-Jones felt she could wash in them, "on to business. We need to understand where we are with regard to current events. Why, Miss Williamson, are you working undercover at Darriby Hall?"

"That's a long story, sergeant."

"Well, we will just have to make time for it as I strongly suspect it has some bearing on our murder case."

"Alright, here goes," Lucy took a deep breath and began. "Our firm was approached by the senior dean at STINK..."

"At what?"

"Oh, that stands for the Science and Technology Institute of North Kakama. You see, the initials are STINK."

"Go on."

"It's a modern university in Washington State, USA, where Professor Hammerstein is based, assuming he's still with us, of course. Well, it all comes down to ownership of the land upon which this spanking new college has been built. You see, it was officially donated to the college by one Denton S. Baron III, but there have been persistent rumours that the land wasn't his to give. Apparently, his forefathers bought it from a local Indian tribe for a wagonload of baubles with a few ancient muskets thrown in."

"Well, that may be immoral or questionable, but what of it? It happened a long time ago," Sergeant Haddock Fisher said, clearly slightly irritated at there being this long-winded diversion when he had a murder to solve.

"Yes, but don't you see?"

"No, dear Miss Williamson, we don't see because, with the best will in the world, you've left out a critical fact."

"Have I?" Miss Williamson looked to Lady Darriby-Jones as if she was searching through endless folders in her mind, ticking off those she felt had been suitably disclosed. "It's my weakest point," she said as the process continued, "briefing people, I mean. That's why I usually work on my own. You see, I was hired to find out the truth of it, the land ownership, I mean."

"That's the missing fact, my dear," Lady Darriby-Jones replied gently.

"Ah, yes, I see now. You need the final piece of the jigsaw, that being who the other contender for ownership is."

"Exactly," said both the interviewers, although Lady Darriby-Jones softened it with a 'my dear' to follow.

"Well, isn't that obvious? Why else would I be here? There's an overwhelming argument to say that Mr Baron, whether the first, second or third, was not the true owner of the land because legal papers say it was purchased by the sixteenth Lord Darriby in 1798 or thereabouts."

"So, it's Darriby land?" Sergeant Fisher was back to aping the haddock, mouth opening and closing as he tried to comprehend what this meant for the case.

Chapter Eighteen

*L*ate September was one of the best times of the year in Lady Darriby-Jones' opinion. But then she thought that about most times of the year; even January had its charms as the crocuses and snowdrops dared venture above ground.

However, this particular late September shone, like the sun, in her memory for many years to come. As she and Lucy Williamson strode back to the house, stretching the limits of Lucy's tighter skirt, they chatted like two schoolgirls.

Except they had a particular concentration on the subject at hand; so more like two schoolgirls trying to cram their history or geography for an upcoming exam.

"So, let me get this straight in the brain department," Lady Darriby-Jones said as they traversed the scene of Barry Baritone's crime. "You were hired by the university. SKINT or..."

"No, STINK," Lucy laughed.

"What a name! They hired you to go undercover at Darriby Hall to try and find out who actually owns the land upon which the university is built?"

"Yes, but it's not just the land that the buildings sit on. There's about two-thousand acres as well, set out as a wildlife reserve."

"Gosh, that's double what we have here, isn't it?"

"No, Lady Darriby-Jones, I think you've got your calculations a bit skew-wiff. I believe you have eight thousand acres here."

"It's still a lot of land to go unloved."

"Oh, apparently, it's very loved and renowned across the USA as a special reserve for all sorts of interesting and peculiar creatures, including, I'm reliably informed…"

"Slugs," Lady Darriby-Jones beat her new friend to the point and then they both laughed as they passed the sluggery to the left and started across the great west lawn towards the hall.

Lady Darriby-Jones had two questions she badly wanted to ask. She came out with both of them, as fitted the direct approach she took to life.

"Miss Williamson," she said, "what did you find out about the ownership?"

"It's Darriby land alright. There's no dispute about that. It was purchased by the sixteenth lord around one-hundred-and-thirty years ago but, you may remember the sixteenth Darriby was a famous frigate captain in the Napoleonic Wars, losing his life suddenly in 1813 when his frigate was attacked by overwhelming odds. He sunk three Frenchies before his own ship went down. It's very sad because the then Lady Darriby was a young woman who was with child, but that baby would only inherit if it was born a boy. Well, it almost didn't happen at all and the poor mother died after the most terrible childbirth."

"And the baby?"

"He was fine, grew up healthy and strong. I do believe he was your husband's great grandfather. The problem is that much of the old lord's affairs were lost and forgotten during the minority of the seventeenth. The American lands were just such; forgotten and the records scattered to the winds. However, in poking about in your library, I discovered the original deed for the purchase of the land and several thousand other acres in other parts of what is now the Western side of America."

"How interesting, Miss Williamson." She strode in silence for a while, then commented that she wondered what her husband would make of it all.

"Technically, you own the university," Lucy said. "That's what the deed says." She drew in her breath to quote from memory, "to include all buildings, however, put up in perpetual ownership of the heirs of Lord Darriby."

"So, let me get this right, my husband is the owner of a university?"

"Correct."

"Which happens to be the centre of slug studies in North America?"

"I believe that statement also to be correct."

"As well as several thousand other acres on the west coast?"

"I can get the exact acreage for you later on... with your permission to look through the records, Lady Darriby-Jones?"

"Granted, my dear, positively granted."

The other question happened to be more personal and took considerably more courage to come up with. Understandable, therefore, that Lady Darriby-Jones didn't breach the subject until the very last part of their walk back from the police station. She told herself that at the mid-point of the lawn she would launch question number two, but they passed this milestone without her raising it. In fact, it's only when her left foot hit the gravel of the drive that she thought, 'it's now or never and I do need to know.'

"Miss Williamson, may I ask you another question, a more personal one?" She punched out her words in time to her foot crunching the gravel.

"Of course, Lady Darriby-Jones. I do believe I know what it is, too."

"Really?" It was a very wide drive but they were making steady progress towards the west entrance, the one that led into the library through a door that did not stick.

"It's why I've been so spiteful and horrid to you during our stay, isn't it?"

Lady Darriby-Jones just nodded; now it was down to Lucy to provide an explanation.

"Orders," she said a moment later, as they exited the gravel and hit the flagstones that surrounded much of the house.

The Mystery of the American Slug

"Orders?"

"Yes, you see, the whole thing about slugs was a cover for me to get into your records and find out what I could concerning the land ownership situation."

"Darriby won't be pleased."

"Oh, don't get me wrong. Professor Hammerstein is potty about slugs, simply loves them. However, there's a level of panic in Washington State that not only have they no ownership, but that the whole university, lock, stock and barrel, is owned by someone else entirely. That sort of takes precedence, don't you agree?"

"I believe so, but why be so antagonistic towards me?"

"That was down to the professor. He wanted me to be invisible, so he decided I should be so caustic and downright rude that nobody would want to be pally with me. I must admit, it sort of worked, didn't it?"

"Yes, I suppose it did," Lady Darriby-Jones replied vaguely, completely overtaken by different and conflicting thoughts. Why go to such lengths unless the intention was to conceal the true ownership of the land, a dreadful act to even consider? Lady Darriby-Jones had been brought up in a coal-mining family, her father having made a very large fortune but still remaining, essentially, a coal miner. He wanted better for his only living child and, consequently, married her into old money. The fact that that old money desperately needed new money was by-the-by. She had adopted her new class instantly and absolutely, falling for the role and lifestyle completely. In the class she had been moved into by her clever father, land ownership was everything. Well, almost so; she, happily, had found tenderness which grew to love, so property probably ran a close second.

And anybody stealing, or attempting to steal, land was a heinous villain without a doubt.

Yet two ironies penetrated her mind as she puzzled on.

First, she liked Lucy Williamson enormously, sensing a kindred spirit, just like young Alfie, who was showing such promise.

Second, her money might have saved Darriby Hall twenty years ago but even it was dwarfed by the ownership of so much land in America, meaning perhaps the Darriby line hadn't needed saving after all.

Chapter Nineteen

The weather turned around at lunchtime. Not terribly so, but a preview of what was to come with autumn threatening to be hard upon them. The wind picked up, blowing clouds across the sun and sending light spatters of rain down across the whole of the Darriby estate.

Lady Darriby-Jones needed to think. Thinking meant walking. Walking meant having a partner, someone to bounce ideas off as they completed circuit after circuit of the house. Her family and friends, seeing the signs, made a quiet arrangement to take turns.

"I suggest ten turns each," Alfie said.

"No, let's make it five at a time," Lady Alice replied. "You go first, then Daddy, then me. I need to fit in a ride this afternoon. I haven't been out all day."

"You're becoming addicted, Lady Alice."

"True," she smiled her reply, "and what are you going to do about it?"

"The only method I've heard that works for addiction is called cold turkey."

"Cold turkey? How would that help?"

"Well, it's not actually eating cold turkey. It's just a phrase for making an abrupt change to your lifestyle in order to get over an addiction. I think it might be American. In your case, it would mean stopping all riding completely and missing it dreadfully but a little less each day."

Alfie's proposal got a snort of derision; she would happily live with her 'addiction' and leave it at that.

Alfie took the first turn, as decided by Lady Alice, but actually looking forward to the detective element of life at Darriby Hall, especially when it involved thrashing ideas around with Lady Darriby-Jones.

Just as they commenced, a car turned in at the distant gatehouse and started to rattle its way up the drive.

"That will be Sergeant Fisher," Lady Darriby-Jones said.

"How can you tell?"

"I was expecting him," she said. "Besides, it's the village police car."

"You can make it out that far away?" Alfie asked, squinting into the distance.

"Eyes like a cat," she replied, wondering if that was the right expression as cats were renowned for their eyesight at night rather than by day.

The Mystery of the American Slug

It was Haddock Fisher and he came with significant news.

"Lady Darriby-Jones," he said, seeing her on the drive and coming straight over to the pair before they had started their first circuit, "I've had a call from the boss."

"He's a little anxious, I imagine?"

"Just the bit of it," he replied. "He's in hot water, that's for sure."

"It's a little unseemly to be seen to take pleasure in the misfortune of others," Lady Darriby-Jones said, "although in this case I believe it has some justification."

"Thank you, Lady Darriby-Jones, if I understood your point properly. Well, you see, he's had a first meeting with the Chief Constable and, the Lord knows what he said, but he still seems to be indicating to the higher-ups that he has the murderer in his grasp."

"And he clearly hasn't," Alfie said. "From what I understand, almost everyone has been ruled out."

"Yes, but it's what the Chief Constable said to him next that matters. First of all, I imagine a fair rollicking going on, but that's none of my business as a lowly sergeant. Well, you see, the Chief Constable has only ordered a press conference for six o'clock."

"A press conference?"

"Yes, to announce the murderer once and for all, Lady Darriby-Jones. I can only imagine that the Chief Constable is fed up of hearing promises in this regard and has decided to step up the pace a bit, putting pressure on the DCI or else exposing him as a fraud."

"Six o'clock? Today?" Lady Darriby-Jones wasn't really questioning the facts, more processing them to try and get some perspective. She started on her first beat around the house. Alfie hung back a little out of respect for the sergeant who followed Lady Darriby-Jones in close order, as if some pearls of wisdom might magically drop from her to him.

But no such pearls dropped and silence prevailed, just the crunch of gravel underfoot and the swish of her skirt as she navigated around the house.

Each time they came around to the front again, Haddock Fisher clearly hesitated, seen in Lady Darriby-Jones' peripheral vision; she thought him wondering whether he should break off this curious procession and return to the station. Or maybe search the hall? His instructions from Manners, as relayed to her by Fisher, were to arrest anyone who seemed a 'half-reasonable fit' for the crime, just to have a body by six o'clock; the guiltier and shiftier the chosen individual looked, the better it would be because the public and the press would believe all the more in that bod's guilt.

But she knew Fisher; for all his casual ways, the sergeant didn't believe in that type of policing, something he called the 'pin it on the first crook you see' approach, based on the assumption that all crooks needed to be in jail so what did it matter if the lines got a bit crossed and Crook A went down for a crime committed by Crook B?

Therefore, she concluded, he stuck to his path, following her footsteps as she considered the matter from every angle.

It wasn't that he was deficient in the head department, just saw things a little more straightforward than others. Hence, good in a crisis, but not so hot when tricky aspects needed working out.

Eventually, Alfie seemed to drop out like a pacemaker in a race, making way for someone else to keep the speed going; except in this bizarre circumstance, the pacemaker led from the rear of the pack.

Five more times around the track, each lap moving them closer to six o'clock. Could they really manage it in time? Nobody wanted to contemplate Manners' 'pin-it' approach, yet Lady Darriby-Jones knew she needed time to find the real killer.

She saw that Fisher had started limping; clearly, his boots were hurting, probably rubbing against the heel. She sensed that he wanted to sit and take the weight off his feet, have a cup of tea and a bun.

Fat chance of that with the marathon continuing. Then, quite suddenly, there was progress, an idea forming in Lady Darriby-Jones' overloaded head.

"Sorry I'm running late," Lady Alice happened upon them at exactly the same time. "Bolter bolted and I had a terrible time catching the rascal. Why are you still here, Alfie? Daddy was supposed to take over from you, not stick to you like a game of follow the leader. Honestly, give a man a simple schedule and..."

"Sssh," said Alfie.

"What's happening?" Lady Alice asked Alfie; for once her father heard and replied that her mother was in thinking mode and best not to disturb.

"Could you ask Miss Williamson to come here?" It would seem that thinking was progressing to action.

"Who?" her husband said, not knowing the intrigue the private investigator had played, pretending to be the wife of Professor Hammerstein. Then a bell rang, somewhere along the corridors of his distant memory. "You don't mean the private investigators Papa hired years ago? Williamson and Sons, yes, I remember them now."

"Yes, Darriby, dear, Mrs Hammerstein is none other than Lucy Williamson, daughter of Gavin, the detective your papa hired and you dispensed with when you took over."

"Couldn't see the point of raking over the past," he said, "too much history in all that. But that's why I recognised the girl, isn't it?"

Alfie ran to fetch the target as soon as he realised who he was seeking and came back five minutes later with her in tow, correctly guessing that the walking party would have carried on, reaching the west lawn by the time they emerged from the house.

"Ah, Miss Williamson, thank you for coming to see me. Would your New York office be open yet? I get confused about the time differences."

Lucy checked her watch, deducted five hours and concluded that 4.15 in England was 9.15 in New York, too early as her brother who ran the New York office was a late riser.

"No," said Lady Alice, who hadn't seemed to be listening to any of the conversation, "you've added five hours instead of deducting it." She used her fingers to illustrate that it was 11.15 in the morning, then stating that any private investigator worth his or her salt should be at their desk by 11.15 in the morning wherever in the world they might be.

"Is he connected to the telephone?" Lady Darriby-Jones asked.

"Yes, we consulted by telephone only last week," Lucy replied.

"Come then," she said, "we've no time to lose. Call Torino, he'll know what to do."

Chapter Twenty

It took a while to get organised, transatlantic phone calls being tricky to organise. Sergeant Fisher led the attack, coming on the phone to the operator and stating it was important police business.

"I still have to book a call," the operator said stubbornly. Then Alfie grabbed the receiver.

"Hello ops," he said, as if he rang up every day. "Can you settle a bet?"

"Well, you're a funny one. What bet would that be?"

"There's £50 on it and a nice bottle of perfume for you. We've got a bet on that we can get a call to New York in the next ten minutes. There's the £50 riding on it but also my hard-won reputation. Do you think you can do it for me, ops?"

"I'll try, sir, hold the line."

Lady Darriby-Jones wondered whether holding the line up in the air might make the words travel more speedily. Or perhaps it shunted others off the line, freeing valuable time for their call.

Whatever it did, Alfie's charm worked a treat. At 4.42pm, a distinct New York accent fluttered on the line, giving the usual:

Williamson and Sons, how may I help you today?

"And daughter," Lucy added crossly.

"Oh my," came the crackling voice, "that wouldn't be Lucy, would it? It's Alma here. Tell me..."

"Unfortunately, we're in a terrible hurry. Can we speak to bro?"

"I think he's in a meeting."

"Can you go in there and call him out?"

It took six minutes to extract Gavin Junior from his meeting and deposit him by the telephone receiver.

"I'll see what I can do," he promised after Lady Darriby-Jones took the phone, introduced herself and spent five precious minutes rambling through the reasons for the call and for the actions they were asking Gavin Junior to do.

"It might be a while," he said in that awkward closing bit of some conversations when nobody knows quite what to say.

They waited and waited then, painfully aware that time was precious and, throw what anchors they could at it, they could never slow it down, not even the Americans could manage that.

The Mystery of the American Slug

Five o'clock came and went, then a quarter past. The clock in the hall clanged once every fifteen minutes. Everyone seemed to be willing the phone to ring before the hall clock gave out the half hour.

When the telephone did ring, it chose the exact same time as the hall clock, such that no one heard it until the echo of the grandfather chimes had receded into the endless corners and winding corridors of Darriby Hall.

Torino had turned up, as if he had a homing signal beating in his brain. It's just as well he did come because he was the more familiar with this 'telephone-thingy', as Lord Darriby-Jones called it.

"Telefono' he called across the study. Before the others realised, he'd picked up the receiver, announcing to whoever might be at the other end that they had arrived at Darriby Hall. "For a Miss Lucy Williamson. It must be a wrong number."

"No," several voices shouted, while even more arms shot out to stop him from replacing the receiver.

"I'm Lucy Williamson," Lucy said, "and that's my bro you've got on the other end of the telephone."

Lucy took the phone and asked for quiet so she could hear what bro said on the telephone. Lady Darriby-Jones ushered everyone out into the hall and told Torino that they all needed drinks, other than the sergeant, because he was on duty, meaning a pot of tea was a necessity. "For me it's the usual," she said, turning back to the study, but noticing that it was now 5.36pm; twenty-four minutes to the deadline. "Actually, Torino, scrap the sergeant's tea. I really think you need to stand by to move quickly when the times come. I'll wait for my pink gin too, if that makes you feel a bit better, sergeant." They were hard up against the deadline.

Inside, Lucy scribbled on a notepad put by the phone for that very reason. Lady Darriby-Jones tried to make sense of her scrawl but couldn't, especially as Lucy was left-handed and one of those left-handers who turned the paper around backwards and placed their hand all over the place to produce a secret script that, presumably, only fellow left-handers could read.

She would have to wait, but felt the clock ticking. How long for the police car to get down the drive with sirens blaring? Maybe eight minutes to the police station? She looked at her watch; eighteen minutes and counting, the second hand moving relentlessly on. Lucy was impossible, discussing some other case with the deadline looming.

All they needed was one piece of confirming information.

Suddenly, there was a nod from Lucy. Frantically, Lady Darriby-Jones signalled back, seeking further confirmation.

After all, it was a big step to take; they had to avoid reasonable doubt, hence the need for absolute confirmation.

Lucy nodded and then gave the thumbs up. It was confirmed. Now Lady Darriby-Jones could spring into action.

Which she did.

"Go go go," she called through the door, opening it just to repeat the same words again. "It's confirmed, sergeant."

"Righto," said the solemn policeman. He too glanced at the clock before opening the library door.

Eleven minutes; they still had an arrest to make. They would never do it. Then, Lady Darriby-Jones had an idea and her smile spread out to encompass everyone around her.

"Miss Betty Bollinger, I am arresting you for the murder of..." Lady Darriby-Jones wasn't listening to the form of words, that being Sergeant Fisher's role. Her responsibility was to follow through on the logistics side of things.

Betty Bollinger had been caught by surprise, no doubt imagining that the bumbling rural police, combined with the equally preposterous amateur sleuth in the form of her host, could never be a match for her ruthless cunning, born of intense anger.

The anger of the dispossessed.

They bundled a confused Betty Bollinger into the back of the police car.

"I'll take the wheel," said Sergeant Fisher, demoting PC Goode to the passenger seat. Even that was denied to him, because Lady Darriby-Jones moved like an agile cat to slip into the passenger seat, just as the engine was starting and Fisher was sliding the car into first gear.

"We'll never make it," Fisher said as he fair flew down the drive, scattering gravel in every direction.

"Not if we go to the police station first," Lady Darriby-Jones replied.

"What are you thinking?"

"Straight to the village hall. It will save two minutes." She looked at her watch. Four minutes to go, just over.

The first thing they saw on approaching the village hall at one minute to six was that there was nowhere to park the car.

"Right there," said Lady Darriby-Jones.

"But that's in front of the Chief Constable's vehicle," Fisher cried.

"We can move it later."

Fisher seemed reluctant, so Lady Darriby-Jones pulled on the handbrake, causing the car to spin around as it slid to a stop.

"Out now," she cried. She opened her door, that of Betty Bollinger as well.

"Step out please, Miss Bollinger."

Betty did as told, appearing the opposite of a murderer in her cute white and orange dress and shiny strap shoes.

Lady Darriby-Jones swung around and stumbled on the kerb, bumping in to a portly fellow.

"Thank you, Lady Darriby," Manners said, "I'll take over now." He frogmarched Betty into the building, turning on the steps to advise Lady Darriby-Jones to go home and have a quiet evening, "Maybe pour yourself a stiff pink gin as a treat."

———

The Mystery of the American Slug

Miss Betty Bollinger, or more correctly, Miss Sophie Baron, was formally charged later that night. She came before the magistrates the next morning and was assigned a lawyer.

Manners came up to the hall at the annoying time of 10.30 that next morning, full of beans at having solved the mystery.

"The Chief Constable was delighted at me presenting the murderer to him ten seconds before the press conference," he said, then demanded coffee and slurped from his cup when Torino poured him some.

"I just have one point of clarification," he said, coffee mostly drunk and wondering why Torino stood immobile against one wall, failing to see a man who needed a second cup. "How on earth did we make the connection?"

"Easy," she replied, right then wanting the rudest policeman in England to be taken down a notch or two. "There had to be a connection with the land."

"What land?"

"Never mind, Mr Manners, I'll put it down in writing so that you can get it typed up as your own report."

"I'd never do that..."

"No, of course not. As I was saying, the land is ours but a body of opinion thought otherwise. Miss Betty Bollinger, now known by her real name of Sophie Baron, was the niece of Denton S. Baron III. Incensed at not being left the land herself by Baron, she decided to take matters into her own hands and wreak vengeance on anybody and everybody connected to the university. She saw this position for secretary to Professor Hammerstein and used her evident charm to get the job, intending to kill and maim as many as she could along the way."

"Little did she know that the land was never her uncle's to give away," Lucy finished the back story just as a vehicle drew up outside.

"Who could that be?" Manners asked, thinking about what other twists there would be for him to get his head around.

"Oh, that will be Professor Hammerstein coming back. Darriby dear?" she called across the room to her husband.

"Yes, dear?"

"It's your turn for the limelight, dear. Are you ready?"

"Yes, dear."

A few minutes later, after the ambulance crew had settled the professor in a comfortable chair in the library, he was most surprised to be addressed by Lord Darriby-Jones, who handed him a handwritten piece of paper.

"Professor Hammerstein, as you suspected, the land upon which your university stands belongs to me as head of the Darriby family."

"Yes, it would seem so," the professor replied glumly.

"It gives me great pleasure to donate that land to a trust for the continued operation of the university in perpetuity."

"What?" The wounded man tried to jump up but couldn't make it.

"On one condition," Lord Darriby-Jones carried on.

"What condition?"

"That the university immediately changes its name from the Scientific and Technical Institute for North Kakama to the Darriby University of Science and Technology."

"That shouldn't be a problem," the professor replied, his relief evident. "But why the change?"

"Simple," Lady Alice's voice carried across the room, "Papa thinks DUST infinitely better as an abbreviation than STINK and, I must say, I'm inclined to agree with him... at least on this one point."

Lady Darriby-Jones chuckled as Manners left and Torino offered more coffee.

"No, Torino, I think I'll indulge myself with an early pink gin, if you'd be so kind."

"Certainly, milady," Torino replied, no doubt wondering what on earth Lady Darriby-Jones would get involved in next.

Life was certainly not boring at Darriby Hall.

The End

Afterword

Thank you for reading The Mystery of the American Slug. I really hope you enjoyed reading it as much as I had writing it!

If you have a minute, please consider leaving a review on Amazon or the retailer where you got it.

Many thanks in advance for your support!

The Mystery Of The Back Passge

CHAPTER 1 SNEAK PEEK

Chapter 1 Sneak Peek

*W*ind howls like a wolf at night, but Lady Darriby-Jones considered there to be no equivalent likeness for the sleet that both thudded to the ground yet came in sheets like curtains across the landscape. Not that she could see out that December afternoon, with dark descended early, but she remembered how it had been all day.

If she hadn't been crossing the hall at the very moment the doorbell rang, intent upon reaching her little private sitting room with endless Christmas planning to do, the resulting mystery may never have surfaced. But she was there. Moreover, too kind-hearted to keep whatever wretch sought shelter from the storm waiting in the cold and the wet, she took on the front door herself. From long experience, she balanced her weight, feet squared, then heaved backwards. The front door stuck horribly and she had been meaning to get something done about it for a long time. But today, it gave way immediately, as if desperate to get the wretch on the outside into the inside, where warmth (at least near the fires that burned in the grates), bonhomie and basic, simple comforts ruled the waves, or whatever they did in English country houses as dusk fell on a frigid December day.

"Good afternoon milady." The voice was familiar, as well as being reassuring, reminding her of the past.

"Good afternoon, Evans." She never had trouble putting a face to a name. Or was that a name to a face?

"So, you do remember me, milady, I thought you would, milady. Says I, 'well Lady Darriby-Jones isn't the one to forget those in need, Evansie, so take heart at the world again; it's not all bad by any means', that's what I says to meself, says I." His words poured forth with evident gratitude. What hit Lady Darriby-Jones, however, wasn't his attitude but his accent; she had once asked which street in Swansea he had come from and had almost squealed in delight when she heard it was less than half a mile from the mansion where she had grown up, and mummy still lived in. Five hundred yards as the crow flies but a million miles in other ways.

"Of course, I do. Evans, Aberdrewgelli Street, number, let me think, 24, I believe." Aberdrewgelli Street was a slum of the first order, nothing much to redeem itself, hence her observation about a million miles yet less than half a mile.

"22, milady, almost spot on, milady. Now, I always says that about the Jones stock. Wherever they find themselves, they have a concern for general kindness that leaves most fellahs standing."

"You'll be wanting something in the kitchen, I suppose?"

"And a bed if you'd be so kind, just for the one night, I'm walking back to Swansea, you see, having been let go from Wayland Towers with not so much as a moment's notice. Quite a horror that's been, see, milady."

"Yes, quite so. Tell me, Evans, who is it in residence at Wayland Towers?" She was playing with him a bit; he probably knew it but played along himself, the game being everything in his world.

"In residence, milady, why it's Colonel Magister, and me being his batman all during the war as well. It's terrible sad how people can change just like that, isn't it so?" He clicked his fingers to emphasise the last point, a spellbinding hypnotic trick that almost worked, except Lady Darriby-Jones knew better from prior experience. She knew, also, that Evans had spent the majority of the war as a guest of his majesty, before doing the patriotic bit for the last three months. Memory of his requested overnight pit stop made her push the pretence a little further.

"Ah, was that the Colonel Magister who married the king's second cousin?"

"That's the one, milady, royalty they are, yet treat good honest men like dirt, says I."

"Well, we will see you right here for a night, Evans."

"Did I say one night, milady? I meant to say..."

"That you're in a rush to get back to your family in Swansea, so can't say a moment longer; yes, it's a sadness we will have to live with. Now, where's Torino? I would take you to the kitchens myself but Mrs Riley will be here any minute and I must find the list of the presents for the children's Christmas party in the village hall. We have to allocate out a present to each child, see? Yes, I know, but we've come to an arrangement with Father Christmas to help at such a busy time. Ah, that must be...no, ah, Alice my dear, could you be so kind as to take..."

"Who's this tramp?" Her quick assessment of the situation seemed remarkable until Lady Darriby-Jones decided that her daughter must have been listening for a few minutes beforehand. Lady Alice squinted towards the pathetic-looking figure, dripping onto the uneven stone floor so that a minute water system was being set up. Lady Alice squinted a lot these days; Lady Darriby-Jones would have to return the favour and take her daughter to that quaint optician in Oxford. "Ah, I see who it is, after the silver no doubt."

"Alice, my dear, I won't have..."

"Well, are you a tramp, Evans? We need the truth now." Alice did interruptions exceedingly well; she always had done and probably always would.

"No, milady, don't you remember old Evansie?" He seemed genuinely upset. "Lady Alice, I used to give you piggy back..."

"What's he want? Where do I take him? Outside, perhaps, with one of my equine whips?"

"Ah, Equine, the best whips always used to be made by Equine and Co, at least before the war. I was a groom to Lord DoNought..."

"I think you'll find his name is Lord Doonay, Evans, but let's not worry ourselves about that just now." Lady Alice turned to her mother and continued talking as if Evans were no longer there, dismissed from the scene. "Mother, if you're asking me to take this wretch all the way downstairs just so the ignorant girls down there can flutter their eyelids as they listen to his ridiculous stories while he helps himself to whatever takes his fancy, then the answer is no. That's spelt 'N' and 'O'; you put them together and get the word 'no'."

"You can also get 'on', milady," Evans decided to add a little spice to the mixture but Lady Darriby-Jones got her metaphors mixed up when she thought that clever quips like that went right up the socks of any Darriby, sadly whether they had a Jones appended to their name or not.

"Please, my dear?" Lady Darriby-Jones had become an expert at daughter-management after nineteen years of practice, sometimes under extreme conditions.

"Oh, very well, if you absolutely insist. Just let me drop this book in the library and I'll take tramp-face down to the kitchens, although he'd be better off with a bit more booze down his throat so he can get that nice room at Darriby Police Station. Well, that's quite the idea, actually." She walked off towards the library door, chuckling about the Darriby Dungeons as she went, something further about Christmas Day and Mrs Fisher's cooking, provided he got the timing just right.

Evans had turned up at Darriby Hall once every eighteen months or so since time began, or at least the last twenty-odd years after Miss Jones had become Lady Darriby-Jones by standing in Darriby Church wearing an expensive white dress, followed by a fun few weeks in Italy getting to know the man who had become her husband. It was on a trip to

Pisa, driving in an open top Rolls from their villa near Florence, that they had stumbled across Torino. She never quite understood how he got a ticket for the same boat train as them, third class instead of first, but the exact same schedule. All she had said to her new husband was something along the lines of how wonderful to have a butler again and what could be better than a foreigner like that kind man we just met, who was looking for employment if the little Italian she had picked up had translated correctly. Somehow it happened and she, being seventeen, ignorant, beautiful (at least in the eye of the beholder), naïve and incredibly wealthy, hadn't gone into any more depth about it except thanking Darriby, her dear husband, silently from time to time for the fascinating psycho-whatever study that an Italian butler in an English country home made.

Thinking of character studies, Lady Alice was not the type to read books, so what was she doing returning one to the library? She looked at Evans, water dripping off him; if her father, Old Jonesy, hadn't made several piles from coal mining, would she be married to someone like him now? Old Mrs Evans instead of Lady Darriby-Jones?

"A penny for your thoughts, Evans."

Evans was a likeable rogue, cadging the necessaries of life from his regular circuit of houses of the rich and once rich. Lady Darriby-Jones knew the elderly spinster sisters who lived at Wayland Towers. The Miss Simpsons would never treat a servant unfairly; if anything the unfairness went the other way.

"I was just thinking of something, you know, from the past, milady." He hesitated, then decided to plunge ahead. "It's just..."

"Out with it, Evans." Whatever it was, it would be fantasy or, at the very least, gross exaggeration; that was the way it was with Evans.

"I don't like to say, milady. You see, there's rumours around that Lord Lowell has escaped from Oxford Prison."

"Good Lord, not Lord..." Lady Darriby-Jones' world closed in, literally; her peripheral vision went, replaced with images of the cruellest, most vicious criminal since Cain laid his brother low. These images taunted her. Nothing could ever be proved against the man who everybody knew killed his cook because the bacon wasn't crisp enough. When his wife, Lady Lowell, had remonstrated with him, she had gone the same way too.

Lord Lowell, a highly able barrister, had defended himself and got away with it, time and time again. Finally, they got him on blackmail charges and he got six years.

It should have been the hangman's noose for what he had done, not least to the Darriby-Jones family, and now he was out, escaped from Oxford Prison, no doubt intent on revenge.

That sent the whole Antarctic of ice up her spine, for it had been Lady Darriby-Jones who had put him there.

And for good reason too.

———

Get your copy of this gripping murder mystery at all good retailers.

A LADY DARRIBY-JONES MYSTERY

THE MYSTERY OF THE BACK PASSAGE

CM RAWLINS

Also By CM Rawlins

A Lady Darriby-Jones Mystery Series

The Mystery of the Polite Man (Book 1)

The Mystery of the American Slug (Book 2)

The Mystery of the Back Passage (Book 3)

The Mystery of the Missing Doctor (Book 4)

Newsletter Signup

Want **FREE** COPIES OF FUTURE **CLEANTALES** BOOKS, FIRST NOTIFICATION OF NEW RELEASES, CONTESTS AND GIVEAWAYS?

GO TO THE LINK BELOW TO SIGN UP TO THE NEWSLETTER!

https://cleantales.com/newsletter/

Printed in Great Britain
by Amazon